"I want you, Tate. Badly."

Linc's big hand covered her cheek and he placed his thumb in the center of her bottom lip.

"I want you, too," Tate admitted. "It's inconvenient and crazy and there are a thousand reasons why it's a bad idea—"

But she didn't have the strength or the willpower to walk away. This one time, she couldn't resist temptation. But, because she had to, she could protect herself. So she did what she always did— she laid out the rules of engagement. That way, there couldn't be any misunderstandings.

"This is a very temporary arrangement, Linc. We're just two adults who are wickedly attracted to each other." This couldn't be anything more and he needed to know that. "This is temporary. So, no expectations, okay?"

"Understood," Linc said.

The fist clenching her heart relaxed. She could do this, and she would be fine. She had to be— anything else wasn't an option.

"So, to spell it out, I look after the kids and you... well, you do what you do. Do we have a deal?"

Linc smiled. "Yes, we have a deal."

* * *

The CEO's Nanny Affair is part of Harlequin Desire's #1 bestselling series,

Billionaires and Babies: Powerful men...wrapped around their babies' little fingers.

Dear Reader,

Jaeger and Beck Ballantyne have both found love and in this Billionaires and Babies book, it's Linc Ballantyne's turn.

Linc has always wanted a big family. He was engaged once, and two weeks before their wedding—six weeks after the birth of their son—his fiancée, Kari, abandoned him and easily relinquished her rights to her son.

Tate is very different from her difficult cousin-slash-adopted-sister Kari, and she finds life easier when she keeps a healthy distance between Kari and herself. Her job as a presenter for a travel program helps her do that. Tate, disappointed by the people who profess to love her, is happy to be a rolling stone, but a request from Kari changes all that. Kari, being Kari, abandons her baby daughter, leaving Ellie with Tate and suggesting she contact Linc Ballantyne to help.

Tate does exactly that but advice is not all she receives from Linc... She also has to deal with his hot kisses and their raging attraction. Both Tate and Linc learn to open their hearts to the possibility of love and they both, eventually, realize that not everything is the way it seems.

I loved writing this book—I have the best job in the world!—and I hope you enjoy Tate and Linc, too.

Happy reading,

Joss

xxx

Connect with me at www.josswoodbooks.com, on Twitter (@josswoodbooks) or Facebook (Joss Wood Author).

JOSS WOOD

—

THE CEO'S NANNY AFFAIR

Recycling programs
for this product may
not exist in your area.

ISBN-13: 978-0-373-83860-8

The CEO's Nanny Affair

Copyright © 2017 by Joss Wood

This edition published by arrangement with Harlequin Books S.A.

For questions and comments about the quality of this book,
please contact us at CustomerService@Harlequin.com.

Printed in U.S.A.

Joss Wood loves books and traveling—especially to the wild places of southern Africa. She has the domestic skills of a potted plant and drinks far too much coffee.

Joss has written for Harlequin KISS, Harlequin Presents and, most recently, the Harlequin Desire line. After a career in business, she now writes full-time. Joss is a member of the Romance Writers of America and Romance Writers of South Africa.

Books by Joss Wood

Harlequin Desire

From Mavericks to Married

Trapped with the Maverick Millionaire
Pregnant by the Maverick Millionaire
Married to the Maverick Millionaire

The Ballantyne Billionaires

His Ex's Well-Kept Secret
Reunited...and Pregnant
The CEO's Nanny Affair

Visit her Author Profile page at Harlequin.com, or josswoodbooks.com, for more titles.

One

Tate Harper had eaten deep-fried crickets in Thailand and snacked on guinea pig in Peru. She'd been lost in a jungle in Costa Rica and danced the night away in a run-down cantina in a Rio favela. She'd been propositioned by both rich and poor men in every corner of the world. As the host of a travel program exploring different food cultures, she'd faced some unusual situations in her life.

But nothing gave her the heavyhearted feeling that a meeting with Kari did.

Tate pushed her fist into her sternum and gripped the handle of the door to the diner. It was a wintry Wednesday afternoon in early January, and she'd touched down at JFK just after six that morning. After already having spent the morning with the executive producers of the travel channel she worked for, discussing her options for hosting a new travel series, she was mentally and physically exhausted. She simply didn't have the energy to deal with her older-in-years-but-still-a-child cousin.

Adopted sister. Whatever the hell Kari was.

Not for the first, or hundredth time, Tate wished that she and Kari were closer, that they were each other's best friends, but, despite she and Kari sharing the same house since she was eight, they'd never really clicked.

That old familiar wave of resentment twisted Tate's stomach into knots. She looked down the snow-dusted road and thought about walking away. She was tempted; her life was so much easier without Kari in it. She shook her head. She wasn't tough enough to ignore Kari's request to meet, and, while she knew she was risking being disappointed for the umpteenth time, a part of her still hoped that they could establish an emotional connection, be a family. Resigned, she pulled open the door to the diner and stepped into its warmth. She shrugged out of her coat, pulled the floppy burgundy felt hat from her head and looked around the diner for Kari. Because their mothers were identical twins, they looked more alike than most sisters did. They shared the same wavy light brown/dark blond hair and long, lean build, but the last time Tate had seen Kari, she'd dyed her hair platinum and was the proud owner of a new, bigger pair of boobs she'd conned someone — probably a boyfriend—into paying for. They also had the same generous mouths and high cheekbones, but Kari had the twins' bright blue eyes while Tate inherited her grandfather's cognac-colored eyes and straight nose.

Not seeing Kari, she caught the attention of a waitress rushing past. "Sorry, excuse me? I'm looking for someone who looks a lot like me. Her text said she was here, waiting for me, but I don't see her."

The waitress nodded. "Yeah, she's sitting at that empty booth. I think she went to the bathroom. Take a seat, she shouldn't be long."

Tate thanked her and walked toward the empty booth, her attention caught by a beautiful biracial baby fast asleep in a stroller parked between the booth and the table next to her, where a couple sat. The baby, Tate decided, had hit the genetic jackpot by inheriting the best of her stunning African American dad's and Nordic mom's genes.

Sitting down, she nodded at the offer of coffee. Hell, yes, she wanted coffee. She wanted to wrap her freezing hands around a warm mug and gaze out the window, happy to be out of the bitter wind and snow-tinged rain. It had been years since she'd been in the city in the middle of winter, and she'd forgotten how miserable it could get.

Next to her, chairs scraped, and Tate turned to watch as the gorgeous man and his blonde partner stood up, gathering their coats and shopping bags. From their intimate smiles and heated looks, Tate realized that they shared a deep connection. Electricity buzzed between them, and she wrinkled her nose as jealously pricked her soul.

She'd never had a man look at her like she was the reason the earth spun on its axis, the pull of the moon on the tides, the strength of the sun.

You've got to be in the game to play it, Harper, Tate quickly reminded herself. *But you chose independence, freedom and to live on your isolated island.* The consequence of that choice was emotional safety.

And, sadly, the sex life of a nun.

But that didn't mean that she couldn't admire a masculine butt in well-fitting jeans. Because he had an A-grade ass, it took Tate a while to realize that they were leaving. Her eyes dropped to the baby still asleep in the stroller, and she shot to her feet. "Hey, wait!"

The couple turned around and they both raised their eyebrows.

Tate gestured to the stroller. "Your *baby*. You're leaving without her."

They responded with frowns and matching is-she-crazy expressions. "That's not our baby. The lady who was sitting there came in with that baby," Sexy Guy told her.

Wait! What?

Tate caught the eye of the waitress as ice flooded her veins. "Who came in with this baby?"

Tate was subjected to another she's-a-nut look. "The woman you asked about, the one who looks like you, she came in with this cutie."

Oh, God, oh, God, oh, God. Tate fought for air and managed to compose herself long enough to ask the waitress if she'd, please, check the bathroom to see whether Kari was in a stall. Tate's eyes bounced between the sleeping baby and the small hallway leading to the restrooms, and when the waitress reappeared, biting her lip and shaking her head, Tate started to tremble.

Déjà vu, she thought. She knew, without a fraction of doubt, that Kari had slipped out the door when her back was turned. *God, Kari, don't... Please don't abandon another of your children. Breeze back through that door, toss me a weak explanation, and we'll pretend this never happened. Just don't walk away; please don't confirm my worst beliefs about you.*

Tate turned around to look at the door to the diner and waited for it to open, waited for the world to stop tilting. When a minute passed and then two, she sighed and turned around again. Feeling moisture on her cheeks, she wiped away her tears and blinked furiously. She wouldn't cry, she wouldn't fall apart. Taking a deep, calming breath, Tate sent another anxious look to the door, hoping for a miracle.

After ten minutes passed with zero miracles occurring, her shock receded, and air rushed into her lungs, clearing the fog from her brain. *Think, dammit. Think.* Legally, this child was her niece, and she was responsible for her. As much as she wished she could run away, her mother had already bolted from the diner, and leaving her alone wasn't an option.

Kari was in the wind… So, what now? Looking down, she saw a diaper bag in the storage area under the stroller, and Tate pulled the heavy sack onto her lap. Resting her arms on the diaper bag, and trying to keep the panic at bay, Tate stared down at the sleeping child.

Angelic, she thought wistfully, because that was the only word that made sense. Her skin was the color of lightly burnt sugar, wispy espresso curls covered her head and her rounded cheeks were pure perfection. The little girl had the wide Harper mouth and pointed chin.

Tate unzipped the diaper bag and peered inside. Seeing a brown envelope flat against the side, Tate pulled it out, her heart hammering. She opened it with shaking fingers, yanked out the papers and slowly flipped through them. There wasn't much besides inoculation certificates and medical cards and a birth certificate stating that the baby was Ellie Harper, the mother, Kari Harper, and father unknown.

God, Kari. How could you not know who the father was? Or did she know and just decided not to inform the state? The last piece of paper was a letter scrawled in Kari's handwriting.

Tate,
I know what you are thinking and I don't blame you. This looks bad; it *is* bad. I need you to take Ellie. Something has come up and I can't keep her. You'll figure out what to do with her.

    If you're freaking out—and you probably are—call Linc Ballantyne, your nephew's dad. His number is below. Ellie is Shaw's half sister and he'll help you out.

I know that you won't believe this but I do
love her.
K.

Her eyes still glued to the letter, Tate shoved her
hand into her bag and pulled out her smartphone.
Feeling like she had a sumo wrestler sitting on her
chest, she entered the phone number and held her
breath as she stared down at the small screen.

What was she doing? Linc Ballantyne's connection to Ellie was tenuous at best—he was Kari's ex-
fiancé and, yes, the father of the now-four-year-old
son she'd abandoned. Linc had lived Tate's current
reality four years ago, and maybe he could help her
make sense of Kari's crazy. It wasn't in her nature
to ask for help, but desperate times trumped pride.

Tate lifted the phone and held it to her ear and listened to it ringing. She was transferred from one efficient Ballantyne employee to another before a deep
male voice muttered a harsh greeting in her ear. As
Linc Ballantyne's sexy voice rumbled through her,
Ellie opened her eyes, and Tate was struck by the
burst of bright, cobalt blue.

Kari's eyes…

"This is Tate Harper, Kari's sister, and I have a
massive problem. Can we meet?"

Some days, running a multibillion-dollar company
gave Linc Ballantyne a splitting headache. Hell, make
that most days lately. Needing an aspirin, Linc walked
into the middle office separating his and his brother

Beck's office, and, ignoring Amy's concerned expression, he pulled out a bottle of aspirin from the top drawer of her desk. He tossed two into his mouth and dry swallowed, very used to the bitter taste.

Amy, the executive assistant he and Beck shared, tucked her phone between her neck and ear and reached across her desk to throw Linc an unopened water bottle. He caught it, cracked the lid and looked through the glass walls to see his still-slim, still-pretty mother walking down the hallway and, as he always did, said a quick, silent thank-you to whatever force that had driven her into the arms of Connor Ballantyne.

Well, not his arms—as far as he knew Connor and his mom were never romantically involved—but into his house, at least. Moving into the brownstone known as The Den and meeting the kids who would become his siblings was the best day of his life; losing Connor, the worst.

Linc hurried across the office to open the door to her and bent down to kiss Jo's cheek.

"Hi."

"Hello, darling," Jo replied. Her eyes were gray, like his, but hers were the color of gentle rain while his were a darker, edgier granite. "I'm sorry to drop in on you without warning."

"That's never a problem," Linc assured her.

Jo greeted Amy with a kiss and a hug, and gestured to his office. "Have you a minute for me, Linc?"

"Always."

In his office Jo sat down as he perched on the

edge of his desk and folded his arms across his chest, feeling the burn in his biceps. He'd pushed himself last night, storming through his late-night workout, hoping that the exercise would ensure a good night's sleep. It had helped somewhat; he'd slept for a solid four hours only to be woken up by Shaw having a nightmare. It had taken an hour to get his son to settle again, and by then he was wide-awake.

"Gary has asked me to move in with him."

Linc jerked his attention back to his mother, trying to contain his shock. "You want to leave The Den? But why so soon?"

Jo rolled her eyes. "We have been in a relationship for more than six months, Linc, so stop acting like I met him two weeks ago! You like him, you told me so."

That was before he was encouraging you to move out, Linc silently groused. Every time Jo mentioned Gary, her eyes glowed and her cheeks warmed. If he believed in love and all that crap, he'd say his mom was head over heels in love with the ex-banker. Since he didn't, he looked past all that and saw two intellectually and socially compatible people who simply enjoyed each other's company. Truth be told, he still didn't like the fact that Jo was choosing Gary over Shaw, the grandson she'd been helping Linc raise since he was six weeks old.

"I think that we'll marry eventually, but I—" Jo continued, rubbing her forehead with the tips of her fingers. "I've lived in The Den for twenty-five years and I love it, but now I want my own home, Linc. I want a place that's all mine, and we want to travel." His mom lifted worried eyes to his. "You know I love Shaw and I was happy to help you when he was a baby because, frankly, you needed the assistance. I still want to help out but—"

"But you don't want to do it every day," Linc said and Jo nodded.

Linc cursed. *Bad time to defect, Mom!* He had a massive company to run and grow. They were re-branding the business, he was considering investing in a diamond mine in Botswana, they had a strike looming at a mine in Colombia, they were opening new stores in Abu Dhabi and Barcelona, refurbishing stores in Hong Kong, LA and Tokyo.

His business life was ridiculously busy and consistently stressful, and he was only able to do what he did because he didn't have to worry about Shaw. His home life ran like clockwork: he took Shaw to pre-K, Jo picked him up and spent the afternoon and early evening with him, feeding and bathing him if he was running late. It worked so damn well because he trusted his mom implicitly, and he never worried about his son's emotional and physical welfare. She was irreplaceable.

"I've been looking after kids for so long." Jo shrugged, lifting delicate shoulders. "I'm nearly sixty, Linc. I want to have some fun, take a break, travel. Have a glass of wine at lunchtime if I feel like it. I'm tired, Linc. Can you understand that?"

Linc stood up and walked to the window, conscious of his accelerated heartbeat and his constricted throat. He hated change, especially in his personal life, and now she'd thrown him for a total loop. Keep calm and think it through. As a father of a mischievous four-year-old and as the CEO of a Fortune 500 company, keeping his head while everyone else was losing theirs was how he navigated his life.

He'd had a lot of practice at being the calm port everyone ran to in a storm. When he was eleven, Jo had secured the position to be Connor Ballantyne's housekeeper and to help him look after his orphaned nephews and niece. His mom told Linc to keep out of the Ballantynes' ways, but Connor, with his huge heart and lack of snobbery, insisted that if they were going to live in The Den, then they had to *live* in The Den. They all ate and played together, and Linc attended the same expensive school as Jaeger and Beck. He read in the library, slid down the banister and peppered the magnificent chandelier in the foyer with spitballs.

To his utter surprise and delight, Connor embraced Linc's presence at The Den, and he never once felt like a third wheel. Maybe that was because Jaeger, Beck and Sage latched onto him, and though he'd been a kid himself, a little less than a year older than Jaeger, he somehow became the person they'd gravitated to. For more than a quarter of a century, he'd been the glue holding the Ballantynes together, and while Beck helped him run Ballantyne International and all four of them held equal shares in the company, he was—despite the fact that he was not a Ballantyne by blood—the leader of the pack.

Linc didn't mind. When he formally adopted the four of them when Linc turned sixteen, Connor made it clear that Linc was the oldest child, that he expected him to look after his siblings, to look after the company, to do him proud.

He had no intention of disappointing the only father he'd ever really known. But Shaw's welfare was his first priority, always. How could he place his son's care in the hands of a stranger? How was he supposed to run this company, nurture and grow it, if he was worried about whether his son was receiving the same attention at home?

Linc opened his mouth to throw himself at her mercy and ask for a time extension but then immediately snapped it shut. As much as he hated change, he couldn't put his needs above Jo's. Especially since she'd dedicated the past thirty-five years putting him first.

Crap. Having integrity sucked.

He turned and forced himself to smile. "So, what do you suggest I do?"

Linc saw the shock and relief in her eyes, ashamed to realize that she'd expected him to argue. "You need a live-in nanny."

Ack. A stranger in his house, looking after his kid. Shoot him now.

"I'll contact the most reputable agencies and select a few for you to interview," Jo said before lifting her eyebrows. "Or do you want to do this yourself?"

Linc shuddered. "No, thanks. I'd rather shower with acid."

His mom cocked her head. "You know what you need, don't you? More than a nanny?"

Sex? A decent night's sleep? A skiing vacation with lots of sex and lots of sleep?

"You need a wife," Jo empathetically stated.

Linc shot her a glare. He so *didn't*. Once upon a time he'd nearly acquired one of those and lost her two weeks before they were supposed to say "I do." For the past four years he'd managed perfectly well without a wife. But he'd had Jo's help... Dammit.

"I've heard all the reasons why you're not interested, Linc. Women are fickle, untrustworthy, they just want your money or the Ballantyne name. Et cetera...et cetera."

"Mom." Linc closed his eyes, looking through the glass wall in Amy's direction. He had a full day ahead, multibillion-dollar decisions to make, and he did not need to talk about his crappy love life. Amy, as she often did, suddenly lifted her head and met his eyes.

"Help me," he mouthed.

"Amy's not going to bail you out," Jo said, not bothering to turn around to look at his assistant. "Besides, she and I agree that you need someone in your life."

"Like I need a needle in my eye," Linc muttered, mouthing "You're fired" at Amy. His assistant just grinned and turned back to her monitor.

"You need someone to challenge you, to make you laugh, to make you think. Someone interesting and independent and smart," his mom insisted.

Why were they even discussing this? Thanks to his ex-fiancée, Kari, he was now determined not to risk his heart, and especially not his son's, on another woman. They were fine on their own. They had to be because there wasn't a woman alive who was worth taking a chance on. He'd learned that lesson well. "Mom, I have work to do. I don't have time to dissect my love life or my relationship with my crazy ex."

Jo stood up and pushed a finger into his chest. "You need to start dating again."

Linc shuddered. Hell to the no. Time to move on. And he could only do that if he deflected the conversation onto one of his siblings. "Talking about relationships, Cady is in Beck's office, right now."

Jo's eyes immediately brightened with curiosity. "Cady? Is she back?"

Linc put a hand on her shoulder and gently directed her to the door. "Amy will explain it to you. I need to get back to work."

Jo glared at him as he reached around her to open the door. "You just don't want to discuss your love life anymore."

"I don't have a love life," Linc corrected, bending down to kiss her cheek. "And I like it that way."

Jo tossed another hot look his way before addressing Amy. "He needs to date."

"I know," Amy answered without missing a beat, her fingers dancing over her keyboard. "I'm working on it."

"You're working on nothing," Linc retorted, "because I freakin' fired you!"

Amy rolled her eyes at Jo, who smiled.

"You're delusional, Linc. We all know that Connor left me in charge. Hold that thought," Amy told him, before answering a call. She listened for a minute before lifting suddenly serious eyes to meet Linc's.

"It's Tate Harper and she needs to speak to you. It's private and, in her words, it's pretty damn urgent."

Linc glanced at his Rolex and glared at the imposing front door of The Den, his brownstone just off Park Avenue that had been in the Ballantyne family more than a century. In the four years since Kari bolted—taking two of his credit cards and her flawless yellow diamond engagement ring with her—he'd had precisely zero contact with the Harper family. He knew that Kari had been adopted by her aunt and had a cousin she'd been raised with, but she had hardly spoken about them.

They certainly hadn't been invited to their wedding, and, at the time, Linc had thought that there was bad blood between them. Now he knew that Kari hadn't bothered with wedding invitations because she'd never intended to marry him. He would've saved himself a bundle in both time and money if the damned woman had let him in on that little secret.

He once thought that she wanted what he did; a home, a family, a traditional family life together, but Kari had run from the life he'd offered her. Most shocking of all, she'd also relinquished all parental rights to Shaw. When she did that he assumed that all connections to Kari and her family were permanently severed, so he couldn't understand why Tate needed to see him.

And why he'd ever agreed to meet with her was equally confounding. But he'd heard something in her voice, a note of panic and deep, deep sorrow. Maybe something had happened to Kari, and, if so, he needed to know what. She was still Shaw's mother, after all.

Linc heard the light rap on the door and sucked in a breath.

The first thought he had when he opened his front door to Tate Harper and raked his eyes over her was that he wanted her. Under him, on top of him, up against the nearest wall…anyway he could have her, he'd take her. That thought was immediately followed by, *Oh, crap, not again.*

Kari had been a stunning woman, but her beauty, as he knew—and paid for—had taken work. But the woman standing behind the stroller was effortlessly gorgeous. Her hair was a riot of blond and brown, eyes the color of his favorite whiskey under arched eyebrows and her skin, makeup-free, was flawless. This Harper's beauty was all natural and, dammit, so much more potent. Linc, his hand on the doorknob, took a moment to draw in some much-needed air.

He scanned her face again, unable to stop drinking in her dazzling beauty. The rational part of his brain wanted him to tell Tate Harper that he had nothing to say to her, no help to offer and that he and Shaw did not need the aggravation dealing with a Harper almost always caused.

The rest of him, led by his very neglected libido—he was a super busy single dad who rarely had time to chase tail—wanted to start stripping off her clothes to unveil what he assumed was a very delectable body.

"Tate? Come on in."

She pushed the stroller into the hall, holding the bar with a white-knuckle grip. Linc, wincing at the realization that he was allowing a whole bunch of trouble to walk through his front door, was about to rescind his invitation for her to step into his home and his life. Then he made the mistake of looking into her eyes and gauged her terror, her complete and utter dismay, and her-what-the-hell-did-I-do-to-deserve-this expression.

She'd jumped into the ring with Kari and had the crap kicked out of her, Linc realized. And, for some reason, she thought he could help her clean up the mess. And, because his first instinct was to protect, to make things right, he wanted to wipe the fear from Tate's eyes.

God, he was such a flippin' asshat.

Annoyed with himself, Linc turned his attention to the occupant in the stroller... Ten or eleven months old, he guessed, clean and well fed. And cute, man, she was cute. He loved kids, and this adorable little one, with those bright blue eyes looking up at him, was born charming. He recognized those lapis lazuli eyes; they were Kari's eyes and this was Kari's kid.

But if this was Kari's kid, then why was Tate on his doorstep with her?

Her hands tightened around the bar of the stroller, no color left in her face. She read the question in his eyes and slowly nodded, devastation glimmering in her eyes as she confirmed his worst suspicions. "She was there, at the place we had arranged to meet. She must have seen me arrive and slipped out when I linked Ellie to her."

Linc placed his hands on his hips and tipped his head back to look at the ceiling. He swore quietly, before returning his gaze back to Tate, who was rocking on her heels. "So, what do you want from me?"

Because I know what I want from you and that's to unbutton that blouse, slide it off your sexy shoulders and feel your silky skin beneath my hands, your made-for-sin mouth fusing with mine. I want to know the shape of your breasts, dig my fingers into the skin of your ass...

Sex? That's where his head went after her shocking statement. What the hell?

For God's sake, Ballantyne, get a freakin' grip! Why, after all the crap Kari had put him through, did he have the hots for her sister?

Linc rubbed the back of his neck. "I need coffee. Would you like a cup?"

"Only if you don't poison it. Or spit in it."

Linc felt his lips twitch and fought a smile. So, she had a bit of a mouth on her. Back in the world he normally lived in, *the one that made sense*, Linc didn't mind sassy women. There was nothing more annoying than someone who agreed with everything he said, so desperate to please. He'd dated quite of few of them.

He didn't like this woman, he reminded himself sternly; he didn't have any intention of liking her, ever. They were going to have coffee, a conversation, and, hopefully, in ten minutes he'd be back at his desk and life would return to normal.

He looked down into the stroller again. "What's her name?"

"In her letter, Kari calls her Ellie."

"Pretty name," Linc said, undoing the harness that kept Ellie in the stroller. He picked her up and placed her on his hip, his arm around her little butt. God, it felt weird, but almost right, to have a baby in his arms again. He'd always wanted a big family, tons of kids. But, since babies usually came with a mother and that species came with complications and drama, he was resigned to being a one-child dad. And that child was pretty damn cool...

"Follow me." Linc led Tate through the second floor of the brownstone and hit the stairs leading to the garden level. Stepping into the large open-plan room, he walked into his, and Shaw's, favorite area of the brownstone—the living room that flowed out from the kitchen and informal eating area. It held long, comfortable couches, a large-screen TV, books and Shaw's toys. Massive French doors led to the enclosed garden with pots of herbs and garden furniture. The rest of The Den held priceless art and rare antiques, but this room was functional, lived-in and cozy.

Linc, still holding the baby, headed to the coffee machine and hit the button to power up the appliance. It was nearly 4:00 p.m., was it too early for something strong and alcoholic? After making coffee, Linc walked back into the sitting area and placed their mugs onto the coffee table.

Tate looked as white as a sheet, shell-shocked and more than a little panicked. She needed to calm the hell down.

"Take your coat off, sit down and breathe," Linc instructed her, relieved when Tate nodded her agreement. In real life, she wouldn't be so quick to acquiesce, Linc mused. It might have been her snarky comment earlier about him spitting in her coffee, but he just knew that Tate wasn't a pushover. It added a layer of intrigue to the sexy.

He watched as she removed her coat, revealing more of that almost perfect body and her glorious blondish-brown hair. "I've lost my hat."

"I think you have bigger things to worry about than a hat," Linc stated, leaning forward to pick up his coffee cup.

Questions that had nothing to do with his ex and her baby jumped into his mind. Would her eyes deepen or lighten with passion? Was she a moaner or a screamer? Would she be...

Linc closed his eyes and forcefully shook his head, reminding himself to start using his brain.

He needed to hear her story so that he could hustle her out of the door and get back to his predictable, safe, sensible world. She was pure temptation, and being attracted to his crazy ex's sister was a complication he most definitely did not need.

"So, start at the beginning and tell me how Kari managed to sucker you into looking after her child."

Two

Tate sank back into the cushions of the super comfortable couch, wishing she could just close her eyes. When she woke up, this would all be a horrible dream, and she'd have a vacation to start, a career to obsess over.

She wouldn't have a baby to think about or to care for, and she certainly would not be in Linc Ballantyne's fabulous mansion on the Upper East Side, looking at Manhattan's hottest and most elusive bachelor.

The photographs of him online and in print publications didn't do this man justice. They simply told the world that he was incredibly good-looking. And by *good-looking*, she meant *fantastically hot*. It was toasty warm inside his house, but she was still shivering, partly from shock but mostly from a punch of "throw me to the floor and take me now."

Under Linc's button-down shirt and tie was a wide chest and, she was sure, a hard, ridged stomach. His shoulders were broad, his legs long and muscular and his short, thick dark hair was just this side of messy. And those eyes, God, his eyes. They were a deep and mysterious gray, a color somewhere between summer thunderclouds and pewter. Short, thick black lashes, a slightly crooked nose and dark, rakish eyebrows added character to his too-sexy face.

But the photographs didn't capture the power sizzling under his skin, the intelligence radiating from those eyes, the don't-BS-me vibe emanating from him. They certainly didn't capture the sheer and unrelenting masculinity of the man.

The man she was fiercely, *ridiculously* attracted to. Of course she was, Tate sighed, because she was a Harper woman and Harper women never made life easy for themselves.

Her eyes moved from his face to the baby tucked into the crook of his elbow, and she swallowed hard. She remembered his earlier question about what she wanted from him, and, not for the first time since stepping into the brownstone, she wondered what she was doing here. She wasn't the type to fall apart in a crisis, who needed a man to sort her life out and she'd learned, at a very early age, not to depend on anyone else to help her muddle through life. People, she'd found, and especially those who were supposed to love her, were generally unreliable.

Ellie was her responsibility, not Linc's. So, really, there was no point in extending this very uncomfortable visit. And the zing of sexual awareness dancing along her skin, making her heart bounce around her chest, added a level of awkward to their encounter.

Tate got to her feet, walked over to him and reached for Ellie, pulling the little girl into her arms. Eleven months old and abandoned, Tate thought. How could Kari do this? *Again*?

"I'm sorry, Linc, we shouldn't have come here." Tate heard her words running together and tried to slow down. "We'll get out of your hair now."

Linc leaned forward and placed his muscular forearms on his thighs, his eyes penetrating. "Take a breath, Tate. Sit down, drink your coffee and let's talk this through."

"I should let you go back to work."

"My day is already shot," he admitted. "Tell me what happened."

Tate gave him a quick rundown of her day, and when she was finished, Linc asked, "Where's the note she left you?"

Too tired to argue, she told him where to find it and sat down with Ellie propped on her lap. Tate took her little hand in hers and thought that Ellie was amazingly docile for a child that had been dumped with a stranger.

"So, though this note is short on details it seems to imply that you now get to call the shots with regard to Ellie," Linc said.

"*Imply* being the *operative* word," Tate bitterly replied. "And what am I supposed to do with her? Look after her? Place her in foster care? Give her up for adoption?"

"I don't think you have the legal right to do the last two," Linc said, and she saw the anger burning in his eyes. "But why couldn't she just do any of this herself? Why involve you?"

"I don't know. I didn't even know about Ellie until I got to the diner. I haven't seen Kari for two years." Tate rubbed her thumb gently over the back of Ellie's hand. "And that meeting was tense."

"Why?"

She started to tell him that they'd had a huge fight because Kari abandoned her son. Tate had been so incensed at her cousin's blasé attitude toward Shaw that she'd stopped communicating with her. Tate noticed Linc's hard eyes and knew that he wouldn't appreciate, and didn't need, her defending his son. Linc Ballantyne was obviously very capable at fighting his own battles.

"Family stuff." Tate eventually pushed the short explanation out.

Linc linked his hands together and leaned back, placing his ankle on his knee and tapping the sheaf of papers balanced on his thigh. "So, what are you going to do?"

Tate forced herself to think. "Right now, I suppose I need to find us a place to stay—"

"Whoa! You're homeless, too?"

Tate glared at him and held up her hand in an indignant gesture. "Hold on, hotshot, don't jump to conclusions. I'm a travel presenter, out of the country for most of the year, so I live out of hotel rooms. Once a year, I get a long vacation, and I came back to New York to meet with my producers. I was planning to find a hotel for a night or two, until I decided where I wanted to spend my vacation. I might have to rethink leaving New York now, since I have Ellie with me."

"Do you have enough cash? She needs diapers and clothes and...stuff."

Stuff. Tate wrinkled her nose. How unhelpful.

She did have enough money. Her living and travel expenses were paid for by the production company, so her hefty salary went straight into her savings account. Kari was a flake, but she wasn't. "Yes."

"You don't seem like you have much experience with babies."

"Or any," Tate replied self deprecatingly. "I'll buy a book," she added.

"God." Linc muttered, shaking his head. "Do you know how to change a diaper at least?"

"I'm sure I can figure it out," Tate huffed.

Linc rubbed the back of his strong neck, above the patch of tanned skin between the collar of his shirt and his hair. It was the dead of winter—why was he tan? And why did she feel the insane urge to taste his skin?

"Are you going to call Child Services and place her into foster care?"

It took Tate a moment to pull her attention back to the conversation...Ellie and what to do with her. *Focus, Harper.*

Tate looked at Linc and saw the wariness in his

eyes and realized that this was a test, that this moment would make him form an opinion of her that wouldn't be easy to change. Wariness and distrust would slide into contempt.

Strangely, she felt the need not to disappoint him, since she felt like Harper women had disappointed him enough already.

This wasn't about him, she chastised herself. It was about Ellie and what was best for her, so Tate tried to imagine how she would feel watching a Child Services officer walking away with Ellie, and she shook her head. "No, I can't do that."

Tate saw, but ignored, the flash of relief that crossed Linc's face.

"I'm on vacation, and I can look after Ellie as well as any foster mother could, once I figure out the basics." She sighed. "I think I need to consult a lawyer and find out whether I can, temporarily, keep her."

He nodded but remained silent.

"Just so you know, I intend to track Kari down and make her face the consequences of her actions. I want her to make the decision to give Ellie up for adoption, not me," Tate added.

"That can be arranged." Linc held her eyes, and in that instant she saw the edgy businessman, the man who made hard, complicated decisions on six continents.

"What do you mean?"

"My best friend owns a security company, but he started out as a private investigator. He tracked down Kari the last time she skipped town. I'm sure he could do it again." Linc's words were as hard as diamonds and twice as cold. Oh, her sister had obviously done a number on this man's head. *Dammit, Kari.*

"I'll think about hiring a PI. But right now I just need to get us settled for the night and meet with a lawyer."

"I'll get Amy, my assistant, to find someone who specializes in family law," Linc said, leaning sideways to pull his ultrathin phone out of his pants pocket.

Tate started to protest but snapped her mouth closed when he issued terse instructions into the phone. God, he sure didn't waste time and was clearly a take-charge type of guy. Would he be like that in bed? Of course he would be; he'd be all "do this" or "do that," and any woman alive would jump to be under his command. Including her. Tate knew, instinctively, that the pleasure he'd give her would be worth any amount of bossiness…

Someone slap me, please, Tate thought. Right… well, Linc wasn't going to take charge of her…in or out of the bedroom.

Tate waited for him to finish his conversation, intending to tell him exactly that. Okay, she might be in his house, having run to him as Kari suggested, but it wasn't his job to fix this.

"No, I am not going to tell you why," Linc spoke into his phone, exasperated. "Jeez, Amy, you don't need to know everything about everybody. Concentrate on your wedding arrangements or, better yet, do some work."

Linc snapped the phone closed and tapped it against his thigh. "I share an assistant with my brother Beck and, unfortunately, she is scary efficient, which leaves her far too much time to meddle in our lives."

Tate nodded, thinking that his crooked smile was charming, the grudging affection she heard in his voice endearing. She should go, she really should. But it was so nice in this warm house, and looking at Linc wasn't a hardship. Tate yawned, fighting the urge to close her eyes. Jet lag and having her life flipped on its head was not a great combination.

Tate fought her tiredness, decided that it was time to leave and was about to stand when she heard the sound of feet on the wooden stairs, the piping voice of a little boy and the measured tones of an older woman. Shaw was home, she thought. Both excited and nervous to meet her nephew, Tate shot Linc an anxious look.

"He knows who Kari is," he told her as he stood and stretched. "I'll explain about Ellie when I think the time is right."

Fair enough, Tate thought.

Tate heard the loud, excited "Dad!" and turned around to see a little boy fling himself at Linc's legs. Tate couldn't help noticing, and appreciating, the way Linc's biceps bulged as he scooped his son up and into his arms, easily holding the three-foot dynamo.

"Dad! You're home! What are you doing here? We made clay dinosaurs at school. Billy made Jamie cry. I fell down and scraped my knee. But I didn't cry or anything."

"I am home, buddy. I needed to meet someone here. I'd love to see the dinosaur you made… Where is it? Who is Billy and why did he make Jamie cry? I'm glad your knee is okay," Linc calmly replied, sending a quick smile to the dark-haired, older woman who walked into the room. "Hey, Mom."

Tate's gaze danced over Shaw's features; he had Kari's blond hair, the same spray of freckles she remembered her sporting in her childhood and Kari's spectacular eyes. Give him twenty years and he would be fighting off girls with a stick.

Shaw must've felt her eyes on him because his head whipped around, and his mouth dropped open with surprise. He wiggled out of his father's arms and belted across the room to stand next to her. "I'm Shaw. Who are you?"

Keep it simple, she thought, seeing Linc's concerned frown. "My name is Tate. And this—" she lifted the little girl's fist "—is Ellie."

Shaw placed his hands on his hips and cocked his head. "Okay. Did you come for a playdate with Dad?"

Tate held back her laugh. Oh, God, she wished that this situation was that simple. "I needed to chat with your dad." She stood up and held out her free hand to Linc's mother. "Hi, I'm Tate Harper, Kari's sister."

Linc frowned. "I thought she was your cousin."

"Legally, we're sisters. My mom adopted her when we were kids," she explained.

Tate expected Jo to give her a very frosty reception, so she was very surprised when the older woman ignored her hand to lean in for a quick hug.

"You're the travel presenter. I love your program! And who is this?" Jo looked at Ellie and shot Tate a sympathetic gaze, and her mouth tightened. "Don't bother answering, I see the resemblance between her and Shaw. She's done it again?"

Tate forced herself to meet Jo's eyes, and saw a mixture of sympathy and anger. Sympathy for her, anger toward her ex-almost-daughter-in-law.

To her dismay, her eyes started to burn with tears. "I flew in from South America this morning. I had a meeting with my bosses. A few hours later and I'm suddenly responsible for a baby!" She waved her free hand in front of her face in an attempt to regain her composure. "Sorry! I'm not a crier but I'm so mad."

"You need a cookie," Shaw said, looking up at her, his expression concerned.

Tate let out a tiny laugh. "I probably do."

"I'll have one with you," the little boy stated, his tone confident. "Then you can feel twice as better."

Linc shook his head, and the amusement in his gray eyes made her heart stutter. "Nice try, mister. You can have an apple, and if you want a cookie, you can have it for an after-dinner treat. That's the rule." Linc placed both his hands on Shaw's shoulders. "In the meantime, you can take your schoolbag upstairs and say hello to Spike."

Shaw nodded and bounded away.

Tate lifted her eyebrows. "Who is Spike?"

"His bearded dragon," Jo replied, shuddering. "Ugly little thing."

Jo reached out and took Ellie from Tate's arms.

Ellie touched Jo's cheek with her little hand, and Jo pretended to bite it. The older woman then turned her megawatt smile onto Tate. "Now, what are we going to do about you two?"

Tate darted a look at Linc and shook her head. "No, really, this isn't your problem. I'll make a plan, figure something out. I'll buy that baby book and muddle along. We'll be fine."

"I think you should stay here tonight," Jo said, her tone suggesting that she not argue. "Judging by your career, I doubt you have any experience with babies—"

"Try *none*," Tate interjected.

"—and I can, at the very least, help you through your first night with her."

Oh, God, she'd love that. Tate knew she could figure it out, eventually, but being shown how to do the basics would make her life a hundred times easier. Then Tate saw Linc's forbidding expression, and her heart sank. He didn't want her in his house or in his life, and she couldn't blame him. The last time a Harper female dropped into his life, she caused absolute havoc and a great deal of hurt. "That's extremely kind of you but—"

"Where are your bags?" Jo demanded.

"Um, still at my company's office," Tate replied, suddenly realizing that if she wanted a change of clothes and to brush her teeth, she'd have to collect the suitcases she'd left in the care of Go!'s security. And she'd have to lug said luggage and a baby to whatever hotel she could find on short notice.

Damn.

Tate straightened her shoulders and injected steel into her spine. She'd faced down bigger challenges than this in cities a lot less sophisticated than New York. She wasn't powerless and she wasn't broke; she'd just have to get organized. "Thank you but no. I'll be fine." She forced herself to meet Linc's stormy gray eyes. "I'm so sorry to have called you. I suppose I panicked."

As Tate went to take Ellie, Jo turned her shoulder away and shook her head. "You're not going anywhere, young lady. You are my grandson's aunt, and I insist that you spend the night. It's not as though we don't have the room."

"Mom—"

Tate heard the warning in Linc's voice even if Jo didn't.

Jo narrowed her eyes at her son. "Linc, arrange for the Ballantyne driver to collect Tate's luggage and have it delivered here. One of those many interns you have hanging around at work can purchase some baby supplies. I'll make a list, and it can be delivered with the luggage."

Linc pulled his hands out of his pockets and lifted his hands in resignation. He looked at Tate and shrugged. "My mother has made up her mind."

But you're not happy about it, Tate thought. She looked at Jo, thinking that she'd try another argument, but Jo's expression was resolute.

"Just for tonight," she capitulated. "Thank you and I do appreciate your hospitality."

Jo walked toward the kitchen, taking Ellie with her. When she was out of earshot, Tate gathered her courage to look at Linc. "I promise you, I won't abuse your hospitality."

Linc nodded, his face granite hard. "I won't let you. Trust me, I have no intention of being played for a sucker again. So, fair warning, whatever you think you can get out of me, it's not going to happen. One night, Tate. That's it. Tomorrow, you're gone."

Tate wanted to explain that she wasn't like her sister, but quickly realized that Linc wasn't interested in her explanations and, worse, didn't care. She was the dust on the bottom of his shoes, and the sooner he could shake her off, the happier he'd be. "Tomorrow, I'm gone," Tate agreed.

"See that you are. My mother got her way this time. She won't again." Linc lifted his wrist to look at his expensive watch. "I've got to get back to the office. I'll arrange to have your luggage collected if you give me the address. Amy's working on finding that lawyer, and I will ensure that whatever my mother wants purchased gets delivered."

"Thank you. I do appreciate your help," Tate said, her back still straight and her eyes still clashing with his.

Linc surprised her when he stepped up to her and gripped her chin in his large hand. An inch apart, she could feel the heat of his hard body, smell his sweet breath. She could see the faint scar in the corner of his mouth, count each individual bristle of his sexy stubble. Her pulse raced. She wanted that mouth on hers...wanted to wind her arms around his neck, to push her aching breasts into his wide chest.

She wanted to know what he tasted like, how he kissed.

"I fell for the machinations of one pretty Harper woman before. I won't do it again." Linc's gaze darted to her mouth and back up to her eyes again. She saw desire smoldering under his layers of anger and frustration. "So don't get any ideas, Tate."

"One night, Linc." It was all she could think of to say, the only words she could force through her lips. "I promise."

Derision flashed across Linc's face as he dropped his hand and stepped back. "Sorry, but Harper promises mean less than nothing to me."

Fair enough, Tate thought as he strode away. If her fiancé had bailed on her and her child two weeks before their much-anticipated society wedding, she, too, would still be furious and not inclined to play nice with his relatives.

And she most definitely wouldn't have been as calm as Linc had remained with her. Tate placed her hands on her hips and stared at her feet.

She'd been granted a reprieve, and she'd use that time wisely to rest and pick Jo's brain on the basics of childcare. Tomorrow she'd move on.

Between now and then the one thing she would not do was fantasize about Linc Ballantyne. Yes, he was insanely hot, but if she were to have a type, he wasn't it. Within ten minutes she'd pegged him as a traditional guy, someone absolutely committed to his son and his family, to his stable, conventional life.

He was everything she was not. And that was perfectly fine with her, because in the morning she would be moving on.

After all, moving on was what she did best.

Three

In the space of an afternoon, Tate had fallen in love.

She absolutely adored her niece, was partly in love with Jo, was pretty much there with Shaw and utterly entranced with the brownstone the three of them called their home. It was after midnight, and Tate, barefoot and dressed in a pair of yoga pants and a T-shirt, padded down the imposing wooden staircase, her hand sliding down the banister. How many hands had repeated the same action since the house was built in the late 1800s? How many guests had snuck down these stairs to head for the kitchen for a late-night glass of milk or a glass of wine to aid sleep?

Clutching a baby monitor, Tate stepped off the last tread and turned into the enormous room on the ground floor. Jo had taken her on a tour of the five-story home earlier in the day, and every room was a delight. The huge entrance hall opened up to reception rooms and formal living rooms, a library and a smaller sunroom.

The second floor was Linc's domain, comprising a master bedroom, a home office/library and Shaw's bedroom and playroom.

She was on the third floor, in the middle bedroom, which was linked by an interleading door to Shaw's old nursery.

Jo occupied the top floor but this ground-level floor was already Tate's favorite. As a food lover, she was delighted by the state-of-the-art kitchen. She loved the way the kitchen flowed into an informal dining area and then into a relaxed living space filled with books and toys and…mess. Magazines and coloring books and handheld computer games. The mess reassured her that a family lived here.

Oh, she did love the house but… What was it about it that made her feel out of place? It wasn't the luxury; she didn't care about the expensive furnishings and the exclusive address. It was the permanence of The Den, Tate realized, that made her feel twitchy. Like Ballantyne's store on Fifth Avenue, their flagship store, it was an institution. It screamed tradition, solidity…everything she, the ultimate rolling stone, was not.

She was a product of her tumultuous past, Tate decided as resentment twisted her stomach into knots. Her life had been perfect before Kari and her mom, Lauren, Tate's mother's twin, came to live with them for what was supposed to be a month or so, until the single mom found a job and her bearings. A month had turned into six, and her dad had moved out, threatening divorce unless their lives returned to a normal, Kari- and Lauren-free existence.

Her mom, Lane, chose her twin. Tate had lost her dad, her home and her mother, who seemed to prefer Kari to her, all in less than a year. They all had lost the financial security her father had brought to the table. Then when she was eight and Kari eleven, her aunt had been diagnosed with breast cancer and quickly passed away, leaving the three of them to muddle along, moving from one rental to another. Lane had managed to scrape enough money together to cover the legal fees for her to formally adopt Kari and to petition the courts to change Tate's surname to Harper, with no objection from her father.

All her life Tate had felt like the third wheel and a stranger in her own house. Her teenage years with Kari had been pure hell. Kari had an uncontrollable temper, a sense of entitlement and was a master manipulator.

Tate had coped by dreaming of running away to places like Patagonia and Santorini, Istanbul and Ethiopia. Anywhere, she decided, was better than sharing a small house with a selfish, irresponsible drama queen and her enabler. When she left home to travel the world, she'd realized her teenage instincts were correct and that she was much happier having an ocean and a couple of continents between her and her mother and Kari. She liked being alone and free, not having to answer to anyone but herself. It wasn't that she didn't like people, she did, but her mom and Kari were emotional leeches. At a young age she'd learned to create little pockets of solitude around herself and tried to spend as much time there as possible.

When you didn't rely on anybody for anything—companionship, love, company—they had no power to hurt you.

It was funny how two melded-together families, hers and Linc's, could be so different. When Kari and Linc had become engaged, Tate made it her mission to study the family her sister was marrying into, and she'd been impressed by what she'd learned from press reports and interviews with various members of the famous family.

Their story was a modern-day fairy tale. Jaeger, Beck and Sage Ballantyne were orphaned young and placed into the care of their uncle, Connor Ballantyne. Linc was the housekeeper's son, but Connor adopted all four children as his, and they were now one of the most powerful and influential families in Manhattan, known for their fierce love and loyalty to each other and the family name. If you messed with one Ballantyne, it was said, you messed with three more.

Their commitment to each other was absolute.

The Ballantynes functioned as a cohesive unit, whereas her family was a train wreck, and her only commitment was to her job and to avoiding Kari. That entailed staying on the move, never allowing herself to put down roots. Without roots and connections she couldn't disappoint people and, more important, open herself up to being disappointed.

Using the light from the hallway, Tate headed for the stainless steel fridge and pulled out a bottle of milk. After opening cupboards she found a glass and sat at the informal table to drink her milk. She'd love a cookie, but she felt that rummaging about in the Ballantyne cupboards was an abuse of their hospitality.

Despite feeling like she was camping in the middle of enemy territory, Tate had enjoyed her evening with Shaw and Jo. It was a relief not to have Linc there, glaring at her as she ate; thank God for whatever it was that kept him at work past dinner and bedtime. Though, possibly, working late was just an excuse to avoid her. Truth or lie, Tate silently thanked him— the evening had been far more relaxed with Jo and Shaw than if she'd had to make awkward small talk with the deliciously sexy Linc.

She'd never understood why Kari walked out on the man. Kari craved status, and Tate had expected her to grab onto Linc like the lifeline that he was. After all, he had been—still was—New York's biggest catch. Seriously smart and successful, devastatingly handsome, filthy rich. And judging by the way that Shaw's eyes lit up when he spoke about his dad, he was an excellent father.

Linc was the type of guy women dreamed about. A full-time, fully involved father. Someone stable, committed, responsible.

Tate had never believed in fairy tales, in handsome

princes and happy endings. But she did believe in the power of lust… It was simple attraction to Linc that made her heart thump, her blood heat and her panties a little uncomfortable. Images of them together, on his huge bed upstairs, bombarded her. She could easily envision herself naked on his sheets, his big body covering hers, his long, muscled legs tangled with hers. Chest to chest, breaths and mouths and hands mingling… Had he loved Kari like that in that same bed?

The thought barreled in from nowhere and Tate groaned. God, she now needed brain bleach to wipe out that thought. They might have made Shaw in that very bed!

Tate scrubbed her face as her heart constricted. She scowled at the unfamiliar sensation. Thoughts of Kari and Linc together made her feel totally off-kilter. Why? Tate didn't like the only, and obvious, explanation. She was jealous; jealous of Kari, envious that she'd had that sexy mouth on hers, his broad hands stroking Kari's skin and not her own. Tate shuddered at the thought of Linc and Kari, naked, doing what naked people did.

You are not allowed to lust after Kari's ex, Tate told herself sternly. It was against the sister code, the cousin code, against the laws of nature.

Besides, Linc was the last guy on earth she should be attracted to. Like his house, he had an air of tradition, permanence, solidity. Kari had informed her—during their awful fight—that she and Linc agreed that she would be a stay-at-home mom, that they would have a traditional marriage, with Linc as the breadwinner. But that was too conventional for her sister, so she'd run.

Like Kari, Tate was a drifter. But unlike her sister, she was determined to keep her distance from people—men!—and she guarded her independence, like a mommy bear guarded her cubs.

She and Linc were noon and midnight, cliffs and sea, trains and planes…

And really, she had bigger problems to deal with than this inconvenient desire to see Linc naked. *Get a* grip *for goodness' sake!* Lusting after Linc was a stupid waste of energy, and, besides, she knew that he would rather kiss Shaw's bearded dragon than kiss her.

She was under no illusion that when Linc looked at her, he saw Kari, and, on the surface, they were alike. But if Linc took the time to get to know her, which he wouldn't, he'd quickly see that they couldn't be more different. She might not have the trappings of wealth, but she had a very healthy bank account, thanks to saving most of her salary for the past seven years. She worked hard, and she was committed to her career and her independence, but those came at a price. On occasion, she was desperately lonely, and sometimes she craved company, someone else to talk to besides her production crew. Sure, she wasn't interested in a relationship, but she sometimes hungered for a connection, a pair of strong arms around her, a masculine chest to lay her head on, a deep voice whispering dirty things in her ear as hot hands explored her body.

She could handle sex, a fling, even a temporary affair—provided there was an end in sight—but her lifestyle, and career, made that difficult. Most of the men she met were backpackers and travelers, and she understood that, for them, hooking up while traveling was a major part of the "experience." Apart from the icky diseases factor, she really didn't want to be another in their long line of sexual conquests. And sleeping with her coworkers was out... As a result, she'd been celibate for more years than she'd care to count.

Linc, damn him, made her remember exactly how long it had been. Why did he have to be such a sexy, sexy guy? He made her remember what being uncomfortably horny felt like. That had to be why she felt like she wanted to jump out of her own skin whenever he was around.

"Can't sleep?"

Tate screeched and hurtled up from her chair, knocking over her glass of milk. She tried to grab the glass, but it rolled away from her, off the table and smashed on the tiles below. Tate swore and, as she put her foot down, she felt a shard of glass pierce her heel. She groaned and dropped her butt onto the chair, hoisting her heel up onto her knee to look at her wound.

Tate blinked when the kitchen filled with light and turned her head to look at Linc, who was walking toward her. She started to apologize for breaking the glass, but her words, and the moisture in her mouth, disappeared when she saw that he was dressed in nothing more than athletic shorts and shoes. Earlier, dressed in his suit, he'd looked urbane and sophisticated, but this Linc—perspiration glinting on his bare skin, bulging muscles, a defined six-pack and muscled thighs—was pure masculine power.

"Sorry, I didn't mean to scare you." Linc said, walking over to her and bending his head to look at her heel. He winced at the shard of glass in her heel. "Can you pull it out?"

Tate quickly removed the sliver and dropped her heel.

"Careful," Linc warned. "There's glass everywhere."

"Sorry," Tate said. "I'll replace the glass."

Linc frowned. "It's a glass, Tate, not a Picasso. Relax. And sit down. I'll clean up."

"But—"

"I'm wearing shoes. You are not," Linc said and turned to walk into the expansive utility room behind the kitchen, returning with a broom and dustpan. Within minutes he'd swept up the glass, mopped up the milk and was chugging down a bottle of water he'd pulled from the fridge.

"Do you normally work out at midnight?" Tate asked, trying to break the heavy silence between them.

Linc lifted a big, broad shoulder, and Tate wondered how it would feel to run her hand through his light sprinkling of chest hair. "I work out daily. Sometimes I have crazy days, and that means that my work-out happens at crazy hours." Linc lowered his water bottle and nodded at the baby monitor on the table in front of her. "Did she go down easily?"

Tate shook her head. "Not really. I had to rock her to sleep." She made herself meet his hard eyes. "She's probably missing Kari."

Linc bent down and rested his forearms on the granite island of the kitchen, his expression broody. "So, have you decided what you're going to do?"

"About Ellie?" Tate clarified and waited for his nod before continuing. "I'm still thinking it through. My plan is still to get legal advice and go from there."

"Are you going to talk to my PI?" Linc leaned his butt against the kitchen counter and crossed his an-kles. His hands gripped the granite countertop behind him, and his muscles bulged and tightened. Raised veins—a fine indication that he was super fit, in case she didn't catch a clue from his zero-fat, all-muscle body—snaked over his forearms and biceps.

Concentrate, Harper!

Tate squirmed under his hard, penetrating stare, sensing that he was frustrated by her lack of deci-siveness. He wanted answers, an immediate plan of action. It was the CEO way, she decided.

But this wasn't his company; it was her and Ellie's lives. She'd take all the time she needed to make a decision she felt comfortable with. Besides, he would be free of them in the morning, so what did he care?

But he'd been kind enough to let her stay here tonight, so she thought she might, maybe, owe him a brief explanation.

"I'm conflicted and feeling a lot overwhelmed, Linc. I need time to process what's happened," Tate admitted, she jumped up from her seat at the table and walked toward him.

So much for a brief explanation, she thought, as words rolled off her tongue. "I know I can't look after a baby, and I don't want the responsibility of making decisions for Ellie. I have two months before I go back on the road and can't take a baby with me! Ellie is her daughter, not mine. I mean, God, she's cute and sweet and pretty damn easygoing but I'm not mommy material!"

How could she be? Lane, Kari, even her aunt Lauren, had been—were—shockingly bad mothers, and there was no reason to think she'd be any different.

Having a baby was the ultimate commitment, so keeping Ellie was out of the question. Besides, conventional wisdom stated that the child was always better off with their mother so restoring Ellie to Kari was her ultimate goal.

"Along with your killer body and gorgeous hair, that seems to be a trait you share with your sister," Linc said, his voice flat.

His words were an acid-tipped arrow straight to her heart. She wanted to lash back, to tell him that she wasn't anything like Kari, that she wasn't irresponsible and selfish and so very screwed up. But the suspicion in his eyes told her that, no matter what she said, he wouldn't believe her.

But she had to try. For some crazy reason she didn't want him to judge her by her family name. She was better than he thought. "I'm not my sister, Linc."

Linc didn't acknowledge her words. He just held her indignant look, and she watched as his eyes turned from granite to a smoke gray. Oh, God, she recognized that hot, masculine look of appreciation, and it had nothing to do with liking her mind or her personality and everything to do with liking the way she filled out a T-shirt.

He was as attracted to her as she was to him. Oh, Lord, what was she supposed to do with that thought, how was she supposed to process it?

The smart reaction would be to walk away, to turn her back on him and hightail it out of the kitchen and up the stairs. Tate wanted to be smart, she really did. But more than that, she wanted to taste him, to press her breasts into his bare chest, to feel that hard, sweaty skin under her hands. She wanted to inhale him, devour him, climb inside him…

An unintelligible curse erupted from Linc's mouth, and his hand shot out to grab her wrist. With a hard yank, he pulled her into him, and her hips slammed against his erection—ooh, nice—and he ducked his head to cover her mouth with his.

He didn't bother to sip or suckle, he didn't tease or taunt; Linc just slid his tongue into her mouth to tangle with hers, challenging her to give as good as she got. Tate responded by twisting her tongue around his, answering his silent dare.

Something hot and hard arced between them.

Tate felt heat zinging through her as Linc's big hand slipped between the fabric of her shirt to cup her, his hand easily covering her small breast. His thumb swiped her nipple, and she made a guttural sound in the back of her throat, rising on her toes to align her mound with his erection, wanting more heat, more hardness.

Her hands, by their own volition, skated up his rib cage, across his chest, flirted with the ridges of his stomach. Linc responded by placing his arm under her butt and lifting her off her toes. It made sense for her thighs to grip his waist, to hook her ankles behind his back, to rub her long-neglected core against his hot-and-hard-as-hell length. She wanted this man. She wanted him in the worst possible way.

She wanted no fabric between them, she wanted them slick and hot…battling to breathe and crazy with need. Because feeling Linc inside her, touching all those neglected, lonely places, was what she needed, craved. Tate thought about asking him whether he had a condom as she pushed her hands down the back of his shorts to thrust her fingers into the hard muscle of his butt. A wave of desperation rose within her. They had to rid themselves of the barriers of clothing, mostly hers, that kept him from sliding inside her, stretching her and filling her.

Words, she needed them, but she couldn't bring herself to stop kissing him long enough to get her point across. Tate swirled her tongue around his, pulling on his bottom lip, but, unlike earlier, he didn't respond. Tate frowned. Taking stock, it occurred to her that his hands had stopped exploring her body, that she was sliding down his big frame, that her toes and then her feet were touching on the cold floor. Shaking her head, she tried to work out why he'd stomped on the brakes.

Had she done something he didn't like? Did he think that she was a wild woman? A slut? Oh, God, did he think he was kissing Kari and suddenly realized that it was her?

Tate shoved her hands into her hair and looked up him, dreading the expression of cool disdain she knew she'd see.

Linc, however, looked calm and in control and not at all like he'd just tried to inhale her. Where did all that passion go? What had he done with all that hot, unbridled desire? Tate looked down and saw that he was no longer rock hard... *That's an amazing amount of control, Ballantyne.*

It pissed her off.

Tate opened her mouth to utter a very snarky comment, but he spoke first. "Ellie is crying."

Tate blinked, trying to make sense of his words. *Who? What? Where?*

"The baby is crying, Tate. You need to go to her."

Through the monitor on the dining table Tate heard Ellie's soft wail, heard the desolation in her muffled cry, and she snapped back to the here and now. Oh, God, the poor thing sounded like her heart was breaking. How long had she been crying? Minutes? An hour? Longer? How long had she and Linc kissed?

She couldn't tell, she'd lost all sense of time, and of reality.

Oh, my God... She almost lost her freaking mind. She'd been a heartbeat away from asking her sister's ex to do her on the kitchen counter!

What must he think?

And more important, what must Ellie think? Did she think that Tate had abandoned her just like her mother? Not wanting to make the little girl wait another minute, Tate whirled away from Linc and sprinted for the stairs.

Yes, she was desperate to get to Ellie, but honesty made her admit that she was equally desperate to get away from Linc. She had absolutely no control of herself around him, and she thanked God for Ellie's interruption. And for his keen ears because she hadn't heard a damn thing.

She'd been deaf, dumb, blind with lust for him...

It was a very good thing, Tate thought as she sprinted up the stairs, that she was leaving tomorrow.

Four

Linc, after a night short on sleep and long on aggravation, hustled Shaw through his morning routine, trying not to think about the fact that he'd been so close to taking his ex's sister on the kitchen counter the night before. He'd been desperate to know if she was as hot and honeyed as he expected, and his hands had been in her pants, about to push the fabric over her hips, when he'd heard Ellie crying. Would he have stopped if she'd slept through?

Possibly. Maybe. Not a chance in hell.

In his bedroom, Linc muttered a curse as he pulled on his shoes. What the hell happened last night? Yeah, he was horny; it had been a while since he'd last got lucky, but, crap, he never lost control like that. Even as a teenager and at his craziest with Kari, he'd never felt so desperate for a woman, so utterly and incomprehensibly caught up in pleasure.

And the fact that he felt this way about his ex's sister just pissed him off. Bloody Harper women. They had a way of turning his life upside down and inside out. But, he was compelled to admit, he hadn't, not once, thought of Kari when he'd been kissing Tate. Thank God, because this situation was weird enough without getting them confused.

And thank God again that Tate was leaving today because he didn't know if he could spend another night tossing and turning and talking himself out of the urge to go to her room and finish what they'd started.

The sooner Tate left, the better. The world could then stop trying to spin off its axis.

She was the exact opposite of the woman he thought that he and Shaw might someday want. On those odd times when he wished that his life had turned out differently, he fantasized about a sexy, funny stay-at-home mother and lover, someone who adored Shaw. Someone who'd put him and his son at the center of her world, someone he'd trust to stay with him, surfing the waves of life with him and never swimming away.

If he ever got to that place where he felt he could trust again, risk again, Linc knew that he'd want someone who believed in traditions, in order, someone who could fit into his life and who looked the part. He wanted a woman who was easy, and he wanted calm, a lake and not a storm-swept sea.

Tate was exactly what he didn't want or need. She'd create waves and whirlpools, the turbulence he tried to avoid at all costs in his personal life. The woman didn't have a conventional bone in her body; her clothes were bohemian, and, according to Kari, they'd had an unstable upbringing. Tate was a modern-day nomad, a free spirit, innately unconventional.

But, God, the way she kissed; it was a goddamn miracle they hadn't set the brownstone and most of the block on fire.

Linc walked into his closet, yanked a tie from his collection and draped it around his neck, fuming over the fact that he couldn't think about Tate and her mouth and knot his tie into his customary perfect Windsor.

He didn't have enough blood in his brain to do both at the same time.

"Dad, hurry up, Granny Jo is making pancakes," Shaw shouted from the doorway to his room.

Linc frowned. "She's up?"

Shaw nodded. "And she's wearing lipstick. Hurry!"

Linc followed Shaw downstairs, wondering what was going on. Jo was not a morning person, and he and Shaw rarely saw her before breakfast. He did the morning shift, Jo took the afternoons and, if he was slammed, the evening shift. Then Linc remembered that she wanted him to hire a nanny...

Crap.

Linc felt his stomach clench and wondered how he was going to solve that problem. He understood her need to spend more time with Gary, and it wasn't an unreasonable request. His mother was entitled to a life that didn't include the responsibility of looking after his son.

But how was he supposed to trust a stranger with his heart and soul? If something happened to Shaw, he'd crumble. He trusted his mom, his siblings, but anyone else? Hell, no. Nobody would ever love Shaw or look after him like he did, but Jo came damn close.

Well, thankfully, he didn't need to figure it out immediately. Better off thinking about it when he didn't have a came-close-to-having-sex-but-didn't hangover, a headache from too much frustration and not enough sleep.

Linc noticed Tate's bags in the hallway, ready to be loaded in a taxi, and his heart bounced off his rib cage. He tasted panic in the back of his throat and briefly considered whether he was losing his mind. He definitely wanted her to leave; she couldn't stay. Tate was cut from the same cloth as Kari, and the fabric was damaged, stained, torn. He needed another Harper woman in his life like he needed a hole drilled into his head.

But, God, she looked good, Linc thought, as he stopped in the doorway to his kitchen. She looked, and Linc spat out a silent swear. *Right.* Tate sat at the kitchen table, bouncing Ellie on her knee as she listened to Shaw telling her about his favorite teacher at school.

"She sounds really nice." Tate ran a hand over Shaw's head, totally engrossed in what he had to say.

Tate leaned forward, her beautiful eyes sparkling with amusement. "And do you have a girlfriend?"

"Yuck." Shaw looked horrified.

Tate laughed, and Linc felt as if she'd punched him in the throat. Her laugh was similar to Kari's, but not. It was full-bodied and genuine and long on amusement and short on insincerity. Ellie, hearing her laugh, waved her hands around and laughed, too.

God, this was what he'd wanted. Laughing kids, a gorgeous partner, Connor's house filled with joy. He'd wanted this...with someone.

But having it with a Harper woman was utterly out of the question.

"Linc, you're here. Excellent," Jo said, noticing him hovering in the doorway. He kept his eyes on Tate's face, and the laughter in her eyes faded along with the color of her skin. Then a blush appeared on her high cheekbones and mortification flashed in her eyes. So she was regretting last night's madness, too.

He still wanted to kiss the hell out of her, suck her nipples, slide his hand between her... *Ballantyne! Pull yourself together!*

Linc headed for the coffee machine and, keeping his back to the room, yanked a cup from the cupboard and punched a button, mentally begging the machine to hurry up. He needed caffeine. Or a brain transplant. Either would do.

Shoving his hand through his hair, he frowned at his mother. "Is there a reason that you are up and making us pancakes?" he asked, ignoring his mother's narrowed eyes at his surliness.

"Yes!" Jo retorted, sounding far too chipper for someone who was not a morning person.

Something about his mother's cat-eating-canary expression made the hair on Linc's neck rise. He lifted a hand and scowled at her. "No." He nailed her with a hard look. "Whatever it is, just no."

Jo pointed her spatula at the table. "Sit down. And maybe you can remember your manners and say good morning to our guest."

How old was he? Ten? Linc shot Tate a look and saw the twitch on her lips suggesting amusement. "Good morning, Tate." He ran his hand over Ellie's soft curls. God, she was cute. "Morning, honey."

Ellie leaned away from Tate and smiled at him, revealing two little teeth. She lifted her chubby arms, so he picked her up and settled her on his hip where she immediately grabbed his tie and wrapped it around her fingers.

"You don't have to hold her," Tate said, sounding subdued.

"I like kids," Linc told her. It was the truth; he did like kids. Babies didn't scare him; he'd raised Shaw from the time he'd been born, and he never once regretted having him in his life. Shaw was the best thing that had ever happened to him. What the hell was Kari's problem pulling this crap twice? Whether Tate decided to track her down or not, he was going to find his ex and force her to take responsibility for her kid.

She'd refused to be part of Shaw's life, and he no longer wanted her to be, but, God, she wasn't giving up this baby without, at the very least, a reality check from him. He owed Shaw's half sister that.

Linc turned to see Jo, holding a platter of pancakes, staring at him. The corners of her mouth kicked up, and she nodded as she approached the table. "You're going to track her down, aren't you?"

Not bothering to issue a denial—his mom wouldn't believe him if he did—he just took his seat at the table and tucked Ellie into the crook of his arm.

"I think that's the right thing to do," Jo said, placing the platter on the table between them. Linc forked up a couple of pancakes to put on Shaw's plate before pushing the platter in Tate's direction.

"You're going to find Kari?" Tate demanded, her eyes flashing a hard-to-miss warning.

"I'm not going to let her get away with this again. It's b..." Linc looked at Shaw and swallowed the swear. "It's not acceptable, Tate."

"I never said it was," she protested. "It's just that I have a problem with you pursuing this. It's my problem." Tate's hot gaze threatened to singe his skin. "I will handle it."

"My PI already tracked her down once. He will again," Linc stated, using his best don't-argue-with-me voice.

"I'll use your PI, but I'll pay for him and I'll deal with him," Tate insisted, adamant. Linc heard the bite in her voice and sighed when he realized that her lifted nose and snotty expression turned him on. Yep, the party was starting to happen in his pants again...

"He's expensive."

"My problem, my money," Tate leaned forward, and he was distracted by her gaping shirt and the fantastic flash of rose-lace-covered breasts and a cleavage he wanted to ravish with his tongue. Ah, damn, he thought as his blood pumped into his penis. Smooth, fragrant skin, her breathy encouragement in his ear, those small hands on his—

"Linc will pay Reame, the PI. And you will pay him back by staying here and acting as Shaw's nanny for the next two months."

Wait! What? Had he really heard what he thought he heard?

"Mom! What the hell?" he demanded, dropping his fork and yanking his eyes off Tate's fabulous cleavage. Ellie let out a squeal at his raised voice, and he gently patted her thigh to reassure her, and she quickly settled again.

"I'm leaving today, Ms. Taylor," Tate said, panic coating her words.

"Call me Jo, darling." Taking her seat next to Linc, she sent Tate a serene smile, but he immediately recognized the determination in her eyes.

"And, no, you're not. You need a place to stay, and you need to spend some time with Shaw. I need to spend some time with my man... We're thinking about flying to the Bahamas for a week. Linc needs someone to look after Shaw." Jo picked up a pancake from the platter, placed it on her plate and, not appearing to have a care in the world, cut a piece off and lifted it to her mouth. She winked at Shaw, who tried to wink back. "It's the perfect solution for everyone."

"No, it's not. That's not going to work for me," Linc stated, in his coldest voice, the one he never recalled using on his mother before.

"It won't work for me, either." Tate said, her voice shaking.

"Well, it works for *me*," Jo replied, still as cheerful as a sunbeam. She looked at Linc, and he immediately noticed the build-a-bridge-and-get-over-it look that was a feature of his teenage years.

"Linc, with your trust issues and your protective streak, it'll take you months to make the decision to hire a nanny and another six to choose one. I choose Tate. She's related to Shaw, she's lovely—"

He knew exactly how lovely she was, but that had no bearing on this conversation. "She knows nothing about kids! She's unconventional and a free spirit and jet-setter!"

Tate glared at him, looking like she wanted to argue, but at the last moment she nodded, surprising him by agreeing. "All true."

Jo looked from Tate and then at him. "What nonsense! Yesterday afternoon, I called her boss, the executive producer, Keith someone, and asked for a reference on Tate."

Tate looked aghast. "You did what?"

Linc groaned. "God, Mom."

"According to her boss, Tate is punctual and easy to work with. As smart as a whip. She writes and co-produces her show and helps out with the logistics. But, best of all, she's utterly reliable."

His mother, Linc thought darkly, could be damn annoying.

"Oh, God," Tate muttered, putting her head in her hands. After a moment she dropped her hands and narrowed her eyes at Linc. "She's your mother, talk to her."

He'd try. "Mom, you can't ambush us like this."

"Just did," Jo replied, and Linc heard the familiar sound of a text message coming into a phone. Jo pulled her cell out of the back pocket of her designer jeans and swiped her finger across the screen. When she looked up again, her eyes glinted with amusement.

"Gary's booked our flights, and we're leaving for the Caribbean at noon. Yay!" Jo stood up and shoved her phone back into her pocket. She grinned at Linc. "Unless you can find another nanny by noon or play hooky from work, Tate's your only option to look after Shaw. And, Tate, stop being stubborn. You need a place to stay, and Linc, while he can be incredibly annoying and bullheaded on occasion, does know what he's doing when it comes to babies. Stay here, spend some time with Shaw, enjoy the house."

Jo dropped a kiss on Shaw's head, then Linc's, then Ellie's before wrapping her arms around Tate's shoulders and hugging her tight.

Linc had to strain his ears to hear her softly spoken words. "This is a good house, Tate. It can heal you if you let it."

Tate watched Jo walk away and rubbed her suddenly throbbing forehead. What had just happened?

She dropped her hand and looked at Linc, whose eyes held the fury of a hundred hurricanes.

"Bloody Jo," he muttered, and the words were barely out of his mouth before they heard the rumble of deep voices in the doorway. Tate turned around and blinked when a petite, stunning woman with long black hair stepped into the room, followed by two tall, well-built, immaculately dressed men. Damn, the Ballantyne men were a sexy bunch.

The room filled with noise as Shaw jumped up to greet his aunt and uncles, flinging himself against hard legs before being boosted up and over rugged shoulders. Linc rolled his eyes and after ribs had been tickled and hair ruffled, he told Shaw to sit down and finish his breakfast. When Shaw resumed his place at the table, Linc glared at his siblings.

"Yeah, you three are exactly what I need right now," he said, sarcasm coating every word.

Tate felt a flutter of nerves and bit her bottom lip, bracing herself for their hostility.

"Pancakes! Sweet." The tallest of the three Ballantyne brothers slid onto the chair opposite Tate and grabbed a plate. He flashed a grin as he forked a pile of pancakes onto his plate. "Tate, right?" he asked her. "The bride of Satan's sister?"

There was humor in his voice, and while his eyes remained wary, he didn't seem to direct any hostility toward *her*. "I'm Tate and you're…Beck?"

Beck waved his fork at his older brother, who took a seat at the end of the table. "Yep. And that's Jaeger and our sister, Sage."

Jaeger nodded a greeting as he pulled out a chair, clasping the ball of Linc's shoulder before he sat down. "You're looking a bit rough, dude."

"You have no freaking idea," Linc muttered, glaring at Tate. She returned his blistering look, silently telling him not to blame this situation on her. This was his meddling mother's idea, not hers!

"Tate?"

She turned her attention to Sage, who stood next to her chair. The young woman held out her hand, which Tate shook. "Hi, there. We understand that Kari has run off again?"

"Yep." Tate flicked an uncertain glance at Linc, who was pouring juice for Shaw. "I take it that your brother filled you in on my situation?"

"We don't keep secrets in this family," Jaeger said, his voice growly. Tate looked at him, and she saw the warning in his eyes, on his face. Mess with my family and I'll take you apart. Tate knew that this wasn't the time to cower, so she held Jaeger's eyes, and eventually, maybe, she saw a flicker of respect cross his face. A faint smile touched his lips, and then he turned to Linc. "So, what's the plan of action? And leave some pancakes for me, Beck!"

"The plan of action was for Tate to leave this morning. She was going to see a lawyer, I'm going to talk to Reame about tracking down Kari—"

"Reame's going to be pissed at doing that again," Sage commented before asking Tate if she could pick up Ellie. When Tate nodded, Sage took the little girl from Linc's lap. Ellie's hand immediately curled into Sage's long black hair, fascinated.

Linc quietly instructed Shaw to run upstairs to brush his teeth. When his son left the room, he turned his still-annoyed eyes back to his siblings. "Jo has thrown a monkey wrench into those plans."

Tate looked down at the table, shocked to see that the massive pile of pancakes had all but disappeared. Obviously Jo had advance warning that Linc's siblings were coming over; either that or she'd invited them. Tate suspected that they were very aware of Jo's plans and, worse, approved of them. "What's she done now?" Sage asked, rocking from side to side, her cheek on Ellie's head.

"Left me high and dry." Linc placed his forearms on the table and closed his eyes. "She's taking off to the Bahamas with Gary at noon, leaving me without anyone to watch Shaw. And I have a crazy afternoon."

"She didn't provide you with an alternate solution?" Beck asked, draining the rest of Shaw's orange juice, his smile hidden by the rim of the glass. Oh, hell, yeah, his siblings knew about Jo's plan. Tate leaned back in her chair and folded her arms, trying to make sense of Jo's machinations, but all she could think about was the Ballantynes' reactions to her. She'd expected them to hate her, to transfer their animosity about Kari to her. But they seemed to want her to stay with Linc, live in this house and act as Shaw's nanny?

Why? What was their agenda?

Jo could offer her the moon to stay, but Tate knew that, while Jo had conned Linc into letting her stay for a night, he wouldn't be steamrollered a second time. No, this would be Linc's decision...

And hers, obviously. So, what did she want to do? Stay here or go? It would be easy to stay, Tate admitted. On a practical level, if she remained at The Den, there was a fully equipped nursery full of baby equipment for her to use, and she could save the expense of buying equipment she'd only need for a month of two, because, really, how long would it take an experienced PI to track Kari down?

Practicalities aside, she did want to spend some time with Shaw; he was Kari's son, and she adored the blond dynamo. She wanted to make up for all the birthdays and Christmases she'd missed with him, maybe do some fun activities with the little guy. And maybe if he came to care for her as much as she cared for him, Linc would let her spend some time with him when she returned to the Untied States during shooting breaks.

But if she stayed in this house, she would be living with Linc, and the chances of finding herself naked with him were stratospherically high. The guy just had to step into the room, and the urge to jump him was strong. Tate closed her eyes, remembering the feel of his lips on hers, his broad, hard hands on her bare skin. She just had to look at him to turn into a raging inferno. Why Linc? Why now? And why, dear God, did he have to be Kari's ex? Why was she even attracted to him? She'd never been a fan of the Mr. Traditional type of guy, the type who expected his woman to run the household and take care of the kids, ending the day by cooking a gourmet dinner. She was *not* that woman.

"Linc, concentrate!" Beck snapped.

Tate jerked her attention back to the present and saw that Linc was staring at her mouth, his fists resting on his thighs, clenching and unclenching.

"Big Brother is rattled," Beck said, amused.

"What was Jo's suggestion, Linc?" Sage asked, her eyes darting from Linc's face to Tate's and back again.

When Linc spoke, his voice sounded weary. "Well, she suggested that Tate take over as Shaw's nanny until I find someone else, someone suitable."

Sage tipped her head to the side. "Why isn't Tate suitable?"

Linc glared up at his sister. "I don't know her."

"You won't know anyone an agency sends, either," Beck pointed out, standing up to head for the coffee machine. He pulled cups from the cupboard, took milk from the fridge.

"Yeah, but they would've done background checks, have references from other parents," Linc said, glaring at her. "Tate arrived on my doorstep yesterday!"

"Some would call that fate," Sage suggested.

"Fate, my ass," Linc growled.

"You do know that I am sitting here, listening to you talk about me?" Tate interjected, feeling her temper start to bubble.

"You need a nanny, Linc," Beck told him, ignoring Tate's protest. "Unless you plan to take some time off."

"I am not leaving my son with a stranger," Linc said, his jaw rock hard.

The new nanny would be a stranger, too, but that pertinent fact seemed to have escaped Linc's steel-trap mind. Tate's hand gripped her coffee cup, reminding herself that throwing the object would accomplish nothing. Unless the cup hit his head and knocked some sense into him.

"No, what you are really saying is that you won't leave Shaw with a Harper," Tate said, pushing herself to her feet.

Their eyes clashed and Linc nodded. "Yeah, I won't leave him with Kari's sister. Just like I wouldn't leave him with your mother.

"Not that she's ever asked to see him," Linc added, his voice bitter. To Linc, who obviously valued family so highly, her mother's lack of interest had to be a knife to his heart. Tate wanted to tell him that her mother was dead, she wanted to put him in his place, but those words died when she opened her mouth to retaliate.

"Stop comparing me to Kari." It took all her effort to keep her voice calm. "I'm not my sister."

"If it walks like a duck…" Linc said, his words deliberately careless.

Tate heard Jaeger's groan. "Dammit, Linc. Stop being an asshat."

Linc threw up his hands, his handsome face dark with suppressed anger. "It's not like I'm making assumptions here, Tate. Kari spoke about you. You never went to college, wanting to travel instead. You missed countless family events because you had something better to do. You can't wrap your head around commitment, and you'd rather have your freedom than stay in one place. You make a habit of quitting jobs and ending relationships on a whim. Knowing all this, how can I trust that you won't ditch my kid if you have something better to do?" Linc linked his hands behind his head as his chest rose and fell in agitation. "He's my life. I'd never forgive myself if something happened to him on your watch!"

This was why she'd kept her distance from her family, why she'd worked so very hard to create another identity. All her life comparisons had been drawn between her and Kari. Linc was just another in a long, long line of people who'd assumed she was just like Kari and condemned her for it.

She sighed. She'd lived most of her life feeling trapped between two worlds—her family's perceptions of who she was and who they thought she should be.

Now, far away from the life she'd left behind, she felt free, like she could finally be who she really was. People either liked her, or didn't, for who she was without reference to Kari. She made it a point to not worry about what people thought about her, to try to live her life on her own terms according to her own truth.

But, unfortunately, Linc's assumptions about her hurt, and feeling hurt annoyed her. She'd known him for a few hours; his opinion shouldn't matter to her.

But, dammit, it did.

Tate, feeling as if she was fighting a riptide, took Ellie from Sage's arms and dropped a kiss on her silken head. Determined not to let Linc, or his siblings, see how upset she was, she tossed her head and gritted out, "You got all your information about me from Kari, yet here I stand, holding her child, the second one she's dumped. I think there's something wrong with that picture."

Tate walked toward the stairs, feeling the acid burn of tears in the back of her throat. At the door, she made herself turn, to look at Linc once more, probably for the last time. "I'll call for a cab, and I'll be gone in an hour. Good luck in your search for a perfect nanny."

Five

As Ellie played at her feet with plastic toys, Tate looked out her bedroom window to the tree-lined street below. Tate watched as Beck swung Shaw up onto his shoulders, the little boy laughing with delight. Sage was walking alongside Beck, and Jaeger stopped to close the wrought iron gate behind him. They were taking Shaw to his pre-K, Tate surmised. The Ballantyne siblings were a close-knit unit, something she and Kari had never managed to be.

She was, once again, alone. Tate looked down at Ellie's dark head and smiled. Well, she wasn't completely alone; for the next few weeks or so she had this precious little girl for company. Tate bit her lip, wondering if she'd ever see Shaw again. She wanted to be part of his life, but whether Linc would allow that was a tenuous possibility at best. However, there was one thing she *did* know beyond a shadow of a doubt. When she restored Ellie to Kari she'd be a constant and consistent presence throughout Ellie's life, whether Kari wanted her to be or not.

Well, as constant and consistent as her travels and job allowed. Shaw and Ellie were her nephew and niece, the only family, apart from Kari, she had. She wanted a better, healthier relationship with them than she had with her sister and her mother.

The Ballantyne crew turned the corner, and Tate realized that it was a bit of a shock to realize how envious she was of them, of the deep love they shared. A part of her wanted to know what unconditional love felt like—how it felt to be supported, to have a backstop, a soft place to fall. Tate shoved her hands into her hair, frustrated with herself. These thoughts were dangerous and counterproductive. Besides, love's favorite sport was to push her heart through a grinder.

"I handled that badly."

Linc's words danced over her skin, and her stomach quivered. As angry and hurt as she was, he still made her feel like she'd been plugged into a source of pure energy. Unable to face him, Tate sat down on the seat built into the window and watched the road below.

"I'm sorry. I was rude and dismissive and judgmental," Linc stated.

Tate lifted her hand to rub the back of her neck and closed her eyes, wishing that he'd just go away. It would be so much easier if she could just wait for the cab in peace, if she could slip out of the door and avoid this confrontation. She realized that she'd hardly spent any time with him, but she was already so sick of him looking at her and seeing Kari.

Hell, he'd probably thought that he was kissing Kari. It was highly possible that his attraction to her had nothing to do with who she was and everything to do with him taking a walk down memory lane.

Out of the corner of her eye Tate watched as he walked past Ellie to sit beside her on the bench, lifting his ankle up onto his knee. "God, I'm exhausted."

Tate felt his broad, warm hand on the back of her neck and turned her head to look at him. She wanted to pull away from his touch but his fingers pressing into the knots in her neck felt amazing. *Not going anywhere, not going to pull away*, her body told her stubborn brain.

"You must be exhausted, too." Linc dug his fingers into the tight cords of her neck, and it took every ounce of determination she had not to moan from sheer pleasure. "Did you sleep last night?"

"Not much, no."

"Me, either," Linc admitted. "Let's talk, Tate. And this time, let's try not to kiss or yell at each other."

They could try, but she didn't know if they'd succeed. Because she still wanted that mouth on hers. If he tried to kiss her she didn't think she could resist him. Embarrassingly, her brain had lost all control over her body…

"Okay."

Linc dropped his hand and pulled his thigh up on

the bench so that he could look at her. "I *am* sorry for earlier. As Jaeger pointed out after you left, I acted like an ass because I don't like change."

"And you don't know me so you don't feel comfortable leaving Shaw with me. It's okay, I get it. It's a big, bad world—I've seen most of it—and I'm thankful that you are a protective dad."

"I appreciate that. It's been just Shaw and me since Kari left."

"Shaw and you and Jo," Tate corrected.

Linc rolled his eyes. "At this moment she's on my hit list, so I'm not talking about her. She did tell me, *yesterday*, that I should start looking for a new nanny, that she wanted to be a grandmother, not Shaw's caregiver. I never thought that she'd pull this, though. *Blackmailer*."

Tate heard the love under his frustration, but his anger was gone. Not sure what to say, she looked down at Ellie, who was babbling to a doll she'd found in the box of toys. "I've called a cab. It should be here soon. We'll get out of your hair."

"I think you should stay."

Tate's jerked, completely astonished. "You want me to stay?" She frowned. "To look after Shaw?"

Linc shrugged. "Maybe." He held up his hand when she opened her mouth to protest. "Just listen, okay? I need a nanny and you need a place to stay. As you said, I don't know you, and when it comes to Shaw, I'm very slow to trust. Your sister—"

"Messed with your head," Tate finished his sentence for him. She shrugged. "I get it, she's been messing with mine all my life. What else did she say about me?"

Tate saw his hesitation and waited for him to speak. "Nothing much more than what I already mentioned. She didn't speak much about you except to say that you were jealous of her."

Tate rolled her eyes. "As if." She looked him in the eye, desperate to get her point across. "I am not my sister. I didn't go to college, but, over the years, I managed to study part-time to get a degree in world history. I did miss many family events, but I also wasn't invited to many. I like being free to do my own thing. That's why having Ellie to look after is a shock. Kari was flat out lying when she said that I quit jobs and end relationships on a whim—I've had the same job for the past six years, and I haven't had a significant relationship to quit, on a whim or not."

Tate just stopped herself from telling him that keeping her distance and remaining independent were essential to her. *Too much information, Harper.*

"Oh, and my mom didn't contact you because Kari told her that you threatened to have her arrested if any of her family tried to reach out. She convinced my mom that you had the power and money to do that."

Linc gripped the bridge of his nose and shook his head. "God, she's a piece of work. I did offer to let Kari have visitation rights with Shaw, but she wasn't interested. But if your mom wanted to meet Shaw, I'd make that happen. Supervised, but it could happen."

Tate's heart bumped against her rib cage at his generosity. "Thank you, but she died a couple of years ago."

Linc squeezed her knee. "I'm sorry, Tate. I wish I'd known…" His voice trailed off. "Anyway, I was wrong to judge you by your sister's actions but she…" Linc rubbed the back of his head, looking uncomfortable. "She ripped the rug out from under me."

"You really loved her," she stated, the familiar mixture of regret, guilt and sadness rolling around in her belly.

"I loved what thought I was getting," Linc gruffly admitted.

"Which was?"

"A complete family, my family within a family. She told me that she wanted to be a mom, a wife, my partner. I thought she would be the person I could come home to, normality after a crazy day."

Tate raised her eyebrows. "You associated Kari with *normality*?"

Linc grimaced. "Very briefly. Anyway," he said, moving the conversation off Kari and the past, "getting back to what we were discussing, you moving in…" He took a deep breath. "Stay for a week, and I'll work from home. I'll help you with Ellie, and you can spend some time with Shaw. If, at the end of the week, I feel comfortable handing Shaw over to you to look after, I'll go back to work and we'll do a trade. I'll feed and house you and pay for the PI, if you look after Shaw until I find a full-time nanny."

Tate considered his offer, quickly running through her options. It was a fair offer, she acknowledged, except for… "I want to see Shaw in the future, I don't want to walk away and never see him again."

Linc's expression softened. "I can make that happen."

Tate nodded her thanks. "Feed and house Ellie and me, and I'll pay for the PI myself."

"He's expensive, Tate," Linc protested.

"I have money, Linc, and nothing is more important to me than restoring Ellie to Kari," she replied, her tone firm.

"Okay, deal. But what if you find Kari, and she refuses to take Ellie back?"

Her heart lurched. God, she couldn't think about that. Not now. "She will. I'll make her."

"I hope you're right," Linc said. "But, because we are talking about Kari, maybe you should have a plan B."

Tate heard the insistent horn of a taxi and looked out of the window, seeing the yellow cab outside. She took a deep breath and nodded. "Okay, deal. One week and we'll reevaluate."

Linc placed a hand on her shoulder as he stood up, squeezing gently. "Thanks, Tate. I'll go down and tell the taxi he's not needed, and I'll bring your bags back up."

She pulled her knees up to her chest, thinking that she shouldn't ask the question burning her brain. But she couldn't stop the words. She had to know. "Linc…?"

He placed his hand on the doorjamb and turned. "Yeah?"

"When you kissed me last night. Were you thinking about Kari?"

Linc released a sound that sounded like a half snort, a half laugh. "No, that was all you, Tate Harper." His dark gray eyes dropped from her face to her chest, and back up to her face again. Then his gaze lingered on her mouth, and his eyes heated as his hands curled into fists. Tate thought that he might be trying to stop himself from reaching for her.

Or was that wishful thinking?

"It was all you," Linc repeated his words, his voice sounding like sandpaper. "*Only* you."

Linc disappeared, and Tate heard him heading down the stairs. "Damn, Ellie."

At the sound of her name, Ellie looked up and gifted her with a gummy grin.

"How the hell am I going to resist him?"

The child, not understanding the question, threw her doll at Tate's legs.

He was living with another Harper woman, Linc grumbled to himself a couple of days later, running down the stairs from his home office to open the front door.

God help him. Kari had been, generally, a pain in his ass, but Tate, well, she was trouble on a whole new level. Because no matter how hard he tried, he couldn't get her off his mind.

And he didn't like it. Not one bit.

Linc looked at his watch and thought that he'd known her for less than three days and every minute they were together he fought the urge to take her to bed. Her perfume was in his nose, the memory of her smooth skin was on his hands, and the image of those warm cognac brown eyes, foggy with passion, were burned into his retinas. He was *so* screwed, metaphorically speaking. Sad as that was.

Stop thinking about sleeping with her, Ballantyne. Think about business and the fact that you are less than useless working from home, mostly because you are so easily distracted by a pair of long, sexy legs and that that tumble of long, wavy hair you want to sink your hands into.

He bit back an oath. Work was piling up, and he couldn't leave Beck to carry the load for much longer. It wasn't fair and it wasn't right. Jo was having a ball with Gary, and Linc knew that he'd lost her as his full-time caregiver; he had to find someone to look after Shaw on a permanent basis.

Tate seemed to be doing okay, he reluctantly admitted. She and Shaw seemed to click, helped by the fact that Tate was able to spend hours with him in the afternoons, building forts and racing cars, Ellie close at hand. After sampling his runny scrambled eggs on day one at Frustration Central, she kicked him out of the kitchen, cheerfully stating that she'd cook. She quickly and with the minimum of fuss, whipped up meals that both Shaw and Ellie could eat and then tossed together a more adult meal the two of them could share while exchanging polite conversation and pretending that they weren't imagining each other naked. So far he'd eaten a Thai curry and a pork-

and-beans dish from the deep South. If she wasn't a Harper, and he didn't want her in his bed, he'd probably employ her on the spot as his housekeeper/nanny.

Lusting after the nanny, such a cliché. And if that thought wasn't enough to dampen his raging libido, then he should remember that she was the last person that he should be interested in. She was a nomad, she'd only be around until she reunited Ellie with Kari, and then she'd shoot off to parts unknown.

She was also his ex's sister, and he'd been burned by one Harper blonde before. Did he really want to risk repeating *that* crappy experience?

If it meant getting her naked then…maybe. But probably not.

God, he was arguing with himself, a new low.

Linc opened the ornate wooden door and glared at Reame Jepsen, his oldest, closest friend and owner of the best investigative company in the city. His green eyes sparkling with amusement, Reame lifted his eyebrows and gave him a knowing look.

"What's up, dude? You look pissed," Reame drawled, walking into the hallway, taking a moment to look at the stained glass windows on either side of the door. "God, I love this house. Always have."

Reame was his one friend who knew him from BC—Before Connor. They'd both lived in the same run-down apartment building in Queens, but, somehow, their friendship survived his move to Manhattan when Jo landed the job of Connor's housekeeper, his subsequent adoption by one of the wealthiest men in the country and his very privileged lifestyle.

Reame had no idea how much Linc admired him; he'd grown up poor, joined the military, served with distinction in the Special Forces and established one of the most respected security and investigative companies in the city.

Reame said that he couldn't have done it without Connor's, and then Linc's, business, but Linc disagreed. His buddy never gave up and never gave in. He would be exactly where he was, with or without Ballantyne business.

"You're wearing your pissed-off-with-women expression," Reame stated, after they exchanged a one-armed, super brief hug.

"Thanks for coming over," Linc told him as they walked deeper into the house, heading for the downstairs family room. Reame shrugged off his thanks, and Linc knew that, like his brothers, Reame would move mountains for him if he needed him to.

"So, who's the woman?" Reame asked, not allowing Linc to change the subject.

Knowing that his friend wouldn't let the subject die, Linc pushed frustrated fingers through his hair. "Kari's sister."

Reame's eyes narrowed with suspicion. "Satan's bride's sister is here? Why?"

"Long story, we'll go into it," Linc said, rubbing the back of his neck. "She's actually going to be your client... I'm just doing the introduction."

Reame shook his head. "Nope. Not happening. I'm not interested."

"Hear her out, Reame. She's not like Kari." Linc hesitated. "At least I don't think she is."

Reame groaned, looking appalled. His fist rocketed into Linc's shoulder. "Are you freaking nuts? What is it with you and these Harper girls?"

"God knows," Linc replied, rubbing his shoulder. "Just listen to her, please?"

"Okay." Reame folded his arms over his chest. "But if I don't like her or what she has to say, or think she's trying to scam you, I'm not taking her case."

"Fair enough," Linc said as they moved farther into the house. They half jogged down the stairs leading to the kitchen and great room. Linc's eyes scanned the room and saw Tate standing by the doors to the garden, looking at the barren winter garden. Her head resting on Ellie's, her hand was patting the little girl's back in a rhythmic, soothing motion. She kept saying that she wasn't mommy material, but for someone who had been thrust into the role a few days earlier, she was doing fine.

And she looked stunning. Unlike the women he dated who looked effortlessly chic and glamorous, Tate looked relaxed. She wore tall laced-up combat boots and gray over-the-thigh socks, and there was a gap of a few inches between her socks and flowy skirt. Her rust-colored sweater showed off one creamy shoulder, and her long wavy hair tumbled down her back.

Linc looked at Reame, saw his hell-yeah, appreciative look and jammed him in the side with his elbow.

His pal nodded slowly before tossing Linc an amused look. "So...wow," he said, sotto voce.

"Tell me about it," Linc muttered. He called Tate's name and watched as she turned around and gave him a quick, hesitant smile. Her gaze moved on to Reame, and her eyes widened, a common reaction. Reame had a Turkish mother and a Danish father, and the combination of olive skin and light green eyes and big, muscular body, resulted in appreciative looks and flirty smiles. Reame's power over women had never bothered Linc before, but seeing Tate's reaction to his friend pissed him off.

Big-time.

"Tate, Reame Jepsen, the PI I told you about. Reame, Tate Harper. Potential client."

He made a big deal of emphasizing the word *client*. Reame had a cast-iron rule about not sleeping with, dating or having a friendship with his clients. Not that he'd allow Reame to make a move on Tate; he'd rip his old friend's face off first.

God, jealous much, Ballantyne?

Tate moved toward them and held out her hand for Reame to shake. As Tate got closer, Linc saw the tears in the baby's blue eyes, the track marks on her chubby cheeks. Ellie, noticing him, leaned forward, waving her arms at him, silently asking him to take her. Linc obliged and cuddled her close, holding her head to his chest. "What's the matter, honey?" he crooned.

Linc raised his eyebrow at Tate who shrugged. "I have no idea," she replied, frustrated. "She's clean, has had a bottle and she ate her lunch."

"This is a new house, new people, and she's probably feeling a little scared," Linc said.

To his surprise, Tate's eyes filled with tears. "I think so, too." She hauled in a deep breath. "That's why I was rocking her."

"It's all you can do." Linc nodded. "As much as she wants, when she wants it."

Tate sucked in a breath, nodded once and sent him a grateful look. She was holding up well, Linc thought, impressed. Most of the women he knew, with the exception of Jo and Sage—and Jaeger's fiancée, Piper—would be whining about how having to look after a baby interfered with yoga or Pilates or a pedicure.

But Tate just sucked it up and did what she needed to do. He admired her for that.

"Let's have coffee," Linc suggested, suddenly uncomfortable. It was one thing to lust after Tate, but he was playing with fire if he started liking her, too.

"I'll get on that," Tate offered, "since you have your hands full."

"Let's talk while you do that," Reame suggested, walking to the counter and pulling out a stool. "I don't have that much time, and it sounds like you have a story to tell."

Tate nodded. "I understand that you located Kari four years ago after she disappeared?"

"Yeah."

"I need you to find her again," Tate insisted, and Linc heard the bitterness in her voice. She sent Reame a determined look. "Find her so that I can take Ellie

back to her, so that I can talk some damn sense into
her. Find her so that I can tell her that she cannot
dump her children whenever she feels like it!"

Tate closed her eyes as if she were suddenly realizing that she was shouting. She pulled in a long breath,
and her chest lifted and fell. When she opened her eyes
again, her anger, her frustration and her embarrass-
ment were visible. She sent Reame an imploring look.
"Please, just find her. For Ellie. She needs her mom."

Reame looked from Tate to Linc and back to Tate
again. He nodded once and held out his hand for Tate
to shake. Her small hand disappeared into his, and
Reame covered the back of his hand with his other,
his face serious. "I'll find her, Tate. I promise."

He would, Linc thought, feeling relieved. His
buddy never made promises he couldn't keep. Linc's
eyes met his, and Reame gave him a sharp nod, as if
to reinforce his promise to Tate. Then Reame's expression changed, and amusement jumped back into
his green eyes and lifted the corners of his mouth.

Tate turned her back to them, busy with the coffee machine, and Linc raised his eyebrows at Reame.
"What?" he mouthed.

Reame gave him a thumbs-up before lifting his
index finger and pulling it across his throat. Linc
quickly interpreted his gestures. Tate was okay, and
he was in so much trouble.

Which was nothing he hadn't already realized.

When Linc returned to the kitchen after seeing
Reame out, Tate sent him a weary smile. She was

exhausted; partly because she felt drained from talking about Kari and the little she knew of her life but mostly because she'd spent the previous night thinking about Linc and their volcano-hot kiss.

"I need to collect Shaw soon," Linc told her. "His pre-K isn't far from here. Do you want to walk with me? It's supposed to snow soon, so we'd better hustle."

Tate looked out of the window to the gray, freezing day. "Have you heard of a cab? A car?"

Linc smiled. "I need fresh air or else I get twitchy. Come on, don't be a girl."

"I *am* a girl," Tate told him, and his gaze darkened. Yeah, when he looked at her with male appreciation in his eyes, she felt intensely feminine and super sexy.

Dropping her eyes, Tate looked from Linc to Ellie, sitting on the carpet at her feet, and back again. "How far is far? Will Ellie be okay in the cold?"

"I'll find Shaw's old snowsuit and I'll carry her. She'll be fine."

Tate nodded and stood up, feeling Linc's hot gaze on her legs. She raised her eyes and caught his smile, the molten desire in his expression. "As much as I appreciate what you're wearing, I strongly suggest that you put on a few more layers or else you will freeze," he told her, his voice bone-dry.

Tate felt her cheeks warm. "I usually follow the sun. I don't have that many winter clothes."

"You look good," Linc murmured, his voice husky.

Tate shoved an agitated hand into her hair, wishing that he'd stop looking at her mouth. Even better, she wished he'd do something *with* her mouth, like kiss it stupid. Their eyes clashed and held, and Tate swallowed, wishing his big, strong arms were around her, that she could taste his breath, count each bristle on his chin. She wanted him to rip her clothes off her, to undo the buttons of his shirt and push the fabric aside so she could touch his chest, explore the hard ridges of his stomach.

"When you look at me like that, it takes every inch of willpower to stop myself from doing exactly what you are asking for."

Tate touched her top lip with the tip of her tongue. "What am I asking? Bearing in mind that I didn't say a word."

"You don't need to speak. Your eyes say it all. You want to see me naked. And more."

Tate didn't bother to play games by denying his very accurate observation. She just met his direct gaze and nodded. "You want to see me naked, too."

"And do more," Linc rasped, jamming his hands into the pockets of his pants and rocking on his heels. "A lot more."

Tate groaned and had to stop herself from flinging herself against his chest and doing what biology was urging them to do. "This is insane!" she muttered. "Do we not have enough to deal with without this crazy thing zinging between us?"

"Seems not."

"We shouldn't be attracted to each other!" Tate cried.

"Yet, we are."

Tate nodded. "But we don't have to act on it."

"We did the other night," Linc pointed out.

"Only because we both thought that I'd be moving on in the morning! I would never have let that go so far if I thought I was staying."

"Honey, you didn't even hear Ellie crying. I did."

Tate glared at him. "I would have. At some point." She pulled in a long breath and raked her hair back from her face. "Linc, it was a momentary madness. It won't happen again."

Linc sent her a hot, frustrated look. "Want to test that theory? I think that once we start, we won't be able to stop, not again."

Dammit, how was she supposed to resist him? Tate didn't know, but her gut told her that she should. Instinctively, she knew that, while sleeping with Linc would be a delightful way to pass the time, the consequences of their actions would be huge. What those consequences were, she couldn't quite discern, but her instinct was telling her that they would be dire.

Feminine intuition aside, falling into a fling with a hot guy should be the last item on her agenda. She had to look after a little girl who was pining for her mom; she had to find her sister and reconnect mother and daughter. She had a career to return to, places to visit, people to meet.

Living with Linc, *sleeping* with Linc, would make this situation too intimate, too much like the fairy tales she'd never believed in. He was like this house, stable, solid and rooted. He was Manhattan royalty, successfully established and easily juggling his roles as a brilliant businessman and an excellent single father.

Whereas she was a transient, someone who could pack light but who carried far too much emotional baggage. She ran from relationships, from commitment, from anything and anyone demanding that she dip below the surface.

Her attraction to Linc scared her, but the fact that she liked his mind as much as she liked his body terrified her even more.

It's imperative you keep your distance, Harper.

Tate bent down and picked Ellie up. "Let's walk, Linc. Maybe if we get to know each other better, we'll realize that we don't, actually, like each other, and this crazy attraction between us will disappear."

"Here's hoping," Linc said, pushing his hands in the pockets of his pants. "But I think we're kidding ourselves if we think this is going away."

Six

Dressed in layers, Tate pulled the front door closed and headed outside, wincing as the bitterly cold air burned the back of her throat. She fought the urge to run back into the warm house behind her.

Too much sunshine has made you soft, Harper. Suck it up.

Tate drew level with Linc, concerned that Ellie wasn't warm enough. She touched her fingers to the baby's cheek, and Ellie sent her a gummy smile, obviously cozy in the snowsuit that Linc had found in the top of Shaw's cupboard. Ellie seemed very happy in Linc's arms, so Tate shoved her bare hands into the pockets of her parka and her chin into the scarf she'd wound around her neck.

Tate felt Linc's hand on her arm, pulling her left,

and she shot him a glance. "Puddle," he explained and she smiled her thanks. Linc stopped and, with his free hand, pulled his knit hat off his head and thrust it at her. "Your lips are turning blue. Put this on."

"Are you sure?"

"You're turning into a Popsicle," Linc muttered as she positioned the hat over her hair, still warm from his head. "Do you want to go back?"

She didn't. The temperature was dropping rapidly, and she couldn't remember the last time she felt this cold, but with a little exercise she'd quickly feel warmer. She wanted to walk with Linc, breathe in the snow-tinged air and clear her head.

"I'll be fine, thanks." Tate pulled her hands out of her pockets and wiggled her fingers. "But I do need to buy some gloves."

He grabbed her hand and, winding her fingers through his, tugged it into the pocket of his leather-and-sheepskin jacket. Warmth from his hand flowed into hers, and she sighed as they walked shoulder to shoulder down the sidewalk. "Better?"

"Better," Tate replied. "How's she doing?"

"Fast asleep."

Ellie, her curls covered by the hood of her snow-suit, rested her cheek against Linc's black cashmere scarf, and her deep eyelashes were smudges against her caramel skin. She looked like a doll, Tate thought, lifting her free hand to gently rub the back of her knuckle across Ellie's cheek. "She's so beautiful, Linc."

He nodded, dropping his head to look into Ellie's

face. "She really is," he said, his voice tender. Tate wondered if any of his employees or business associates knew that the strong, powerful CEO of Ballantyne International could be brought to his knees by a sleeping baby. "It's cold, Tate. We need to walk."

Her hand still in his, Tate felt grateful when he shortened his long stride to accommodate her shorter legs. Feeling a lot warmer and almost content, Tate rested her head against Linc's shoulder and tasted snow in the air.

What would Kari think if she knew that she was walking hand in hand with her ex-lover, the father of her son? Would she care? Would she think it one big joke? Or would she be jealous as hell? Tate recalled that Kari had never liked to share. When she'd moved in with them after her mother's death, Tate's room became hers, Tate's clothes and toys became hers. Kari, and what she wanted and desired, came first.

No, her sister would definitely not like the idea of Tate cozying up to Linc.

Well, tough. It was her idea for Tate to go to Linc, her decision to abandon her daughter, just like she'd abandoned her son. Kari could shove her jealousy and her what's-mine-is-mine-and-what's-yours-is-mine attitude straight up her—

"Whoa, I can practically see steam coming out of your ears," Linc said. "And you're squeezing the hell out of my fingers."

Tate winced and sent him an apologetic look. "Sorry. Thinking about my sister sends my blood pressure skyrocketing."

"I can relate," Linc stated bitterly.

She gave his fingers a gentle squeeze. "I really am sorry for what she did to you and Shaw, Linc. I was out of the country, but I was furious with her. Nothing I said could change her mind. I tried to talk some sense into her, I promise."

Linc nodded his head, a fine mist on his dark hair. "I appreciate that. I can forgive her for leaving me, God knows that I'm not perfect, but leaving Shaw? Bailing on our son is what I can't forgive. I can't abide people who don't, or won't, shoulder their responsibilities."

Tate heard a note in his voice that suggested Kari wasn't the first person in his life who'd disappointed him. "Who else bailed on you?"

Surprise followed by annoyance flashed across Linc's handsome face. *Bingo*, Tate thought. "You don't have to answer the question if you don't want to. I was just being nosy."

"It was a long time ago, Tate. BC."

"BC?"

"Before Connor."

"That was a long time ago," Tate commented. "It had to have been a hard knock because I can tell it still hurts."

Tate fell quiet, not wanting to push him where he didn't want to go. Not that she could push Linc Ballantyne. She didn't have that much power over him. Or any at all. "My dad walked out on my mom and me when I was five," Linc said, staring straight ahead. His voice deepened when he was upset, Tate realized. Or when he was feeling emotional. "We'd been Christmas shopping. We bought him a pair of golfing gloves." He choked out a small laugh. "Funny the things you remember."

"You came home from Christmas shopping..." Tate prompted, wanting him to finish the story.

"And he was gone. He cleared out their joint bank account and his clothes and vanished. Never to be heard from again."

Tate grimaced. "Your mom couldn't track him down?"

"Tracking someone down takes money and, pre-Connor, there wasn't that much floating around."

He had so much, yet he still remembered how it felt to be poor, Tate thought, amazed. Needing to thank him for opening up, she decided to repay him by doing a little of the same. "I can, sort of, relate. My parents divorced, and my dad faded from my life, and he seemed to forget about me when his new wife got pregnant. After my half brother's birth, I ceased to exist."

Linc pulled his hand from hers to run it through his hair. "One hundred and one ways to screw up your kids."

"You seem to be doing a great job with Shaw," Tate murmured, blowing air into her hands. Linc noticed and pulled her hand back into his pocket.

"Thanks to Connor and Jo."

His tone suggested that he was done with this conversation, so Tate decided to switch gears. "Getting back to Kari, she's always been..." Tate hesitated.

"Selfish? Narcissistic? Self-involved?"

"All of the above," Tate admitted. "I was eight when she came to live with us—"

"Because her mom died?" Linc interjected. He shrugged, and Ellie moved up and down his chest. "Kari didn't talk about her past and would never discuss the future. It was one of the many things that drove me nuts."

She and Kari were alike in that way. Tate rarely opened up about her childhood and torturous teenage years, and as for the future? She didn't make plans beyond the next year or two. That was a Harper trait.

But Linc deserved an explanation. He needed to know who Kari really was, what drove her and why she acted like she did. One day he would have to explain to Shaw why his mom left him, and she never wanted Shaw or Linc to think that they were at fault.

Tate explained how Kari ended up with them and about her aunt's death. "My mom and her twin were exceptionally close, and when she passed away my mom turned all her energy onto Kari, nursing her through her mom's death."

"And where were you in all this?" Linc asked gruffly. Tate jerked her head back, surprised that he'd asked. She'd told this story a few times and most people immediately and, rightfully so, empathized with Kari losing her parent at such a young age.

But Tate also lost her mother at the same time; she'd moved from being Tate's mom to Kari's.

"Lost," Tate quietly admitted. "Kari lost Lauren and I lost Lane. Everything changed that autumn."

Linc's fingers tightened against hers, and in that small gesture she felt comfort and sympathy. It gave her the courage and strength she needed to continue. "My mom created a monster in Kari, something she would never admit. I had to toe the line, but Kari, because she'd lost her mom, was given a free pass. At eleven she was a brat, by thirteen she was uncontrollable and at sixteen, she dropped out of school and moved in with her twenty-four-year-old boyfriend."

"I never knew any of that. I thought she went to college, studied art." He shrugged, his eyes bleak. "I met her at an art gallery."

Tate stopped to look up at Linc, and she felt the frown between her eyes. "Do me a favor? Whatever Kari told you, take it with a very small pinch of salt."

"Did she travel to Europe? Spend some time modeling in Paris? Did she work in Hong Kong in the marketing department of an upmarket clothing company?"

Tate didn't answer. Of course she hadn't, and Linc knew it. Instead of answering, Tate shoved her hands back into the pockets of her parka and shrugged. "In her defense, she probably believed in every lie she told you. For a while, until her attention was caught by something or someone more interesting than you—and by *interesting* I mean *edgier, dangerous, illegal*—she bought into her own lies."

"Yeah, what do they call people like that?" Linc muttered as he snapped his fingers, pretending to think. "Oh, yeah...sociopaths."

"I just want you to know that it wasn't anything

you did or said. Or what you didn't do or say," Tate explained. "Kari isn't the type to stick around."

Linc's steel-gray gaze pinned her to the spot. "Are *you* the type that sticks?"

Tate bit her lip and looked down the wet street. Was she the type to stick? No, thanks to her tumultuous past, she'd shut down and retreated into her own world. She was intensely wary of commitment, of risking her heart. And, like her mom and sister, she wasn't good with routine, with traditions, with rules and regulations. That was why she'd chosen a career that gave her plenty of flexibility and a lot of different experiences.

"I don't stick." Tate lifted her chin and looked into Linc's eyes. "That's why I can't take care of Ellie, why I can't take full responsibility for her. It's not who I am, not what I want to do. I need to be free."

A sad smile touched the corners of Linc's mouth. After a minute of tense silence, he lifted his hand to rub his thumb over her bottom lip.

"At least you're honest, Tate." Linc looked across the road to a brightly painted purple door, and Tate followed his eyes. To the side of the door she saw the discreet sign stating that this building was home to ChildTime.

Even Tate, who had little to no knowledge of kids and schools, had heard of the most expensive and exclusive pre-K in the city. Of course Shaw would attend this pre-K; she kept forgetting that his father was a Ballantyne, one of the most influential and respected businessmen in the city.

She was also finding it difficult to remember that he probably would, in a week or so, be her boss. She would be, officially, his nanny. They had a deal.

And, really, sleeping with her boss—in any capacity—would be so very tacky. Of course, her long neglected libido and her common sense didn't give even half a hoot.

Tate, one hand on Ellie's stroller and the other holding Shaw's hand, heard her phone ringing in her pocket and knew that the call would be from Linc. *Again.*

It would be his fourth call in ninety minutes, and Tate debated answering. But, genetically unable to ignore a ringing phone, she sighed with resignation and pulled her phone out of her pocket.

She rolled her eyes at the name on display. Yep, Mr. Paranoid was checking up on her. Over the last week or so, they'd found some sort of routine. Linc took Shaw to school, and then he went to the office, leaving midafternoon to collect Shaw from pre-K. At The Den, they shared a cup of coffee, and then Linc went into his home office to work while Tate took charge of the kids.

They both spent a lot of time thinking about what making love would feel like. Well, Tate knew she did. Far more than was healthy.

But today was different as Linc had called around lunchtime to ask whether she could collect Shaw from school, stating that he couldn't get away from his desk. He then called her forty-five minutes later to remind her to collect Shaw, and then Amy, his assistant, called her to check that she was on her way. The man had serious trust issues, Tate thought. Then again, he *had* lived with Kari, so she couldn't blame him.

Tate looked at her still-ringing phone. There was no doubt that Linc wanted to know that she had Shaw.

Knowing that the call was about to drop, Tate finally answered. Linc's voice, deep and sexy, but holding a trace of anxiety, flowed into her ear. "I didn't think you were going to answer."

Tate rolled her eyes. "Hi, Linc."

"I'm just checking to see if the school released Shaw to you without any problems. They are sticky about who picks up the kids and when."

Tate decided to have some fun with him. "Oh, God... Is that the time? Was I supposed to collect him? Is it really half past three?"

There was a long beat of silence. Linc was probably deciding whether she was messing with him or not, or he was making plans to put a hit out on her so Tate handed her phone to Shaw. "Say hi to your dad."

"Hi, Dad!" Shaw said into the phone, always happy to talk to Linc.

Linc spoke, and Tate's eyes hit the back of her skull when she heard Shaw's answer. "Yes, Tate was waiting for me when I came out. No, I didn't have to wait for her. Oh, and Dad? I need a lot of cupcakes for tomorrow. Like, *hundreds*."

Tate heard Linc's loud groan and bent her fingers at Shaw, gesturing him to hand the phone over. Lifting the phone to her ear, she pushed the stroller with one hand and headed for home. "You sound like you are about to have a coronary, Ballantyne. I have your kid and we're heading home."

"Did you hear what he said about cupcakes?" Linc demanded, and Tate could imagine him running his hands through his hair.

Okay, this wasn't a big deal. "There are about a million bakeries in Manhattan. Send one of your minions to buy however many you need. Easy peasy."

"Nothing about ChildTime is that easy." Linc growled. "Hold on a sec. I'll see if they sent an email about this."

Tate pushed the stroller and idly listened to Shaw talking animatedly to Ellie as she waited for Linc to come back on the line. When he did, there was tension in his voice. "Yep, I found it. It was something I thought Jo would handle, so I ignored it. And, as per usual, they've complicated the process. They would prefer the twenty-four cupcakes to be homemade, preferably with the child being involved in the process."

"So buying the cupcakes is out."

"Yep, the school actively promotes families spending time together. Crap, I need this like I need a hole in the head. I have this damned photo shoot tonight, and the family is coming over for supper, and I now have to make cupcakes! Shoot me already."

"Twenty-four?" Tate demanded. "How many kids are they feeding?"

"They are asking for extra so that they can donate them to shelters for abused women and kids."

That's a nice gesture, Tate thought, slightly mollified. "What photo shoot?" she asked, recalling his previous comment.

"Our PR expert has the four of us in a series of print advertisements, all of us dressed the same and holding a piece of jewelry or a gemstone we have an emotional connection to," Linc explained. "The idea is to get people to the website to read up on our stones and the story behind them, hoping that they will see something they like on the site and part with their cash to have it."

Tate remembered seeing the ads featuring Jaeger. She'd done exactly what he'd mentioned—she'd read up on how he'd proposed to Piper with the Kashmir sapphire featured in his ad. "It's such a great idea. Is the campaign working?"

"Yeah, we've had good responses to Jaeger's and Beck's ads," Linc replied.

Shaw tugged on her sleeve, and she looked down to see his worried expression. He was four, and he wanted to take cupcakes to school. Tate sent him a reassuring smile.

"Hold on a sec, Linc, while I talk to Shaw." She turned to Shaw and asked, "What if I make the cupcakes and you and Dad decorate them? Would that work?"

Shaw nodded enthusiastically. "Can we make animal cupcakes? Or space monsters?"

Oh, dear Lord. What had she got herself into? Animals? Space monsters…? Well, with the aid of the internet, hopefully she'd figure something out.

"Is that okay with you, Linc?" Tate spoke into the phone again.

"I know you can cook, but can you bake?" Linc asked in her ear, his tone doubtful.

Tate pulled a face. She was a travel and food journalist and a fairly good chef, so whipping up a batch of cupcakes wouldn't strain her culinary repertoire.

"Can you? And more important, do you want to try and fit making twenty-plus cupcakes into your very busy afternoon and evening?" Tate pertly replied.

Linc's sigh was heavy. "No, I can't and, no, I don't."

Tate smiled. "Then your part-time, fill-in nanny will make them."

"My part-time, fill-in nanny is about to get a huge raise."

"I'm sure we can work out a repayment plan that would be a lot of fun," Tate replied, lowering her voice seductively. God, what was she *doing*? She heard Linc's swift intake of breath and knew that she was playing with fire. Tate slapped her hand against her forehead and groaned. She had to resist him, and she should not be making flirty comments!

"What, exactly, did you have in mind?" Linc asked, his voice low and husky and vibrating over her skin.

Tate closed her eyes, mortified. "Ignore me, I should not have said that."

"Why is your face red?" Shaw demanded. "Are you sick?"

Tate heard Linc's wicked laugh in her ear. "Are

you blushing, Tate? What, exactly, are you think-ing about?"

"I am not about to tell you that!" Tate admitted, lifting her hand to her burning cheeks.

"Spoilsport. But it's okay because my imagination is vivid enough for both of us. I'm just glad I'm alone and sitting behind a desk." Linc admitted.

Tate blushed again at the visual that popped into her head and wished that she were with him, touching him, running her hands over the hard-ridged muscles of his stomach and into the back of his pants to push her finger tips into the hard muscle of his butt.

"We can't do this, Linc. We really can't compli-cate our lives by having—" Tate glanced at Shaw "—doing that!"

"I know that. I've tried everything to talk myself out of taking you to bed, but I want you, Tate. I'm wrong for you, and you're wrong for me, but hell… I keep thinking of the patterns I want to draw on your skin, how I want to go about discovering every per-fect inch of you. Then I want to make love to you until you forget your own name."

Oh, God, her panties just caught fire. Tate felt the throb of desire start in her womb and spread through her body, causing sparks to ignite under her skin.

"You're diabolical," she wailed. "This isn't a good idea, Linc. You know it's not!"

"Screw good ideas," Linc muttered.

Thinking that she'd plow the stroller into a light pole if they continued with this conversation, Tate tucked her phone between her neck and jaw, gripped the handle of the stroller with one hand and tightened her grip on Shaw's hand. She had children to get home, cupcakes to make; she wouldn't manage either if she kept fantasizing about the naughty things she wanted Linc Ballantyne to do to her.

They couldn't. They shouldn't.

They *wouldn't*.

"Do you have the ingredients for the cupcakes?" she asked him, thinking that they really needed to get to safer ground.

"Changing the subject, Tate?"

"Absolutely. Let's be smart and keep things simple, Linc."

Tate clearly heard his frustrated sigh, and when he didn't respond she chose to believe that he agreed with her. "So, about those ingredients?"

"I have no damn idea what is in the pantry," Linc eventually replied. "I'll get Amy to send an intern shopping for whatever you might need."

"Flour, eggs, icing sugar, food coloring," Tate rattled off. "Don't go overboard. And do your interns do any real work or are they just there to make your life easier?"

"Both," Linc said. "I'll try and be home as soon as I can. If I'm not home by five, can you let Cady and the photographer into the house?"

"Yep. And I'll even send you a text message to tell you that we are home safe, just so that you have one less thing to worry about," Tate told him.

"Thanks, Tate," Linc said. "I know that you think I'm overreacting and being paranoid but he's—"

"Your life. The reason the sun rises every morning," Tate said softly. God, she'd never been that to anyone, not even to her mom. For Lane, her first, most important connection was to her twin, then to Kari, who was all she had left of Lauren. And then, miles behind, was Tate.

What would that feel like, to be the object of Linc's fierce devotion? His love? Pretty damn awesome, Tate decided. Fully fantastic.

"Tate?"

"Hmm...?"

"You and me? We can try to keep resisting each other, but I suspect it's going to happen and when it does, we're going to blow the damned roof off."

Seven

By five that afternoon, Tate felt like she'd run the New York Marathon, fought off an alien invasion and gone ten rounds with a heavyweight boxer. Twenty-four cupcakes were cooling on the rack, Shaw had a sugar high from licking the sides of the mixing bowl, and Ellie needed her diaper changed. After today, she'd gained a newfound respect for stay-at-home moms and child minders. This job was *not* for the faint of heart.

Tate settled Shaw in front of the TV to watch his favorite show, then crossed the room and picked Ellie up from her playpen. The little girl's hand bounced off her lips, and Tate kissed her fingers. Ellie's laugh, deep and husky, just like Kari's, rumbled across her skin, and Tate cuddled her close, burying her nose in her silky curls. God, she was pure magic, utterly sweet and ridiculously good.

Looking toward the kitchen, she winced. Shaw had insisted on helping her bake, and the kitchen looked like it was ground zero in the flour wars. She still had to pack the dishwasher and sweep the floor, and then they had to decorate the cupcakes.

Tate cast a dark glance at the three massive bags of supplies sitting on the dining table. If Linc's intern had merely sent over some icing sugar and food coloring, they could just top the cupcakes with icing and a sweet. But, no, despite Tate's earlier request, the Ballantyne intern had gone way overboard. There were cutters and stencils, edible flowers and iced animals. Decorating the cupcakes was not going to be a simple affair.

Ellie wiggled in her arms and gave a little wail to remind Tate that she was both dirty and hungry. Tate dropped a kiss on her grumpy lips and, after telling Shaw to leave the cupcakes alone, walked up the steps to the first floor. As she turned the corner, she heard the front door open, and people spilled into the hallway, led by Jaeger Ballantyne, who was carrying a little boy not that much older than Ellie.

"Hey, Tate," Jaeger said, standing back to hold open the front door. "Rough day?" he asked, his expression amused.

Before she could answer, a slim woman walked up to her and leaned forward to drop a quick kiss on her cheek. "I'm Piper. I've been looking forward to meeting you." Piper put her hand on the little boy's thigh. "This is Ty, our son."

"Hi," Tate said warmly, as more people drifted into the hall, including Beck, Sage and a harassed, petite brunette holding a clipboard.

She exchanged greetings with Linc's siblings and watched as Beck grabbed the brunette's arm.

"Cady, meet Tate. She's..." Beck sent Tate a puzzled look. "What are you?"

"A friend of the family. Also Linc's part-time nanny," Tate replied, holding her hand out for Cady to shake. Not wanting to go into her convoluted history with Linc, she nodded to a harassed-looking man dressed in solid black. Behind him, two young women looked equally stressed.

The photographer and his assistants, Tate figured.

"You look like you have your hands full," she said, addressing Cady.

Her back to the photographer, Cady rolled her eyes. "You have no idea." She glanced at her watch and frowned. "We've all had a long day, and Jose is on a tight schedule. I presume Linc is upstairs, dressing?"

Tate pulled a face. "Uh...that would be a no. He's not home yet."

Tate's statement was met with a series of groans, the loudest of which was from Cady. "Seriously?" Beck asked, placing his hands on his trim waist.

"Seriously," Tate replied.

Cady released a strangled moan and scowled at Beck, who threw up his hands. "What? I am not my brother's keeper."

Cady drilled a finger into his flat stomach. "Find him. I have Jose here for the next two hours, and I need to nail this down."

Piper, carrying two grocery bags, lifted them into the air. "And Jay and I will get supper going."

Tate winced. "Uh, sorry. The kitchen is in a bit of a mess. I've been making cupcakes for Shaw to take to school tomorrow. I'll just change Ellie, and then I'll clean up. Can you give me five minutes?"

Sage stepped up to her and took a very willing Ellie from her arms. "I'll change Miss Gorgeous here, if that's okay with you?"

"She's a bit of a mess," Tate warned her.

"I lived with Linc and Shaw and Jo for years. I've changed many diapers. We'll be fine," Sage assured her and headed up the magnificent staircase, crooning to Ellie as she did so.

Right, okay, the kitchen. Tate was about to follow Piper and Jaeger downstairs when the front door banged open, and Linc stepped through the entrance. His eyes immediately clashed with hers, and Tate felt her skin tingle as his stormy eyes roamed over her face, down her long-sleeved T-shirt. His gaze heated, and Tate was quite sure that her panties were about to catch fire.

"Hi."

"Hi back." Tate forced the words up her throat and wished she had the right to step into his arms, to lift her face to be kissed, to feel his big hands in her hair, changing the angle so that he could kiss her with hot abandon.

"You look—"

Stunning? Gorgeous? Sexy? Doable? She'd take any of the adjectives.

"—like you were dunked in a vat of flour."

Tate glanced down at her shirt and saw the streaks of flour and the blobs of batter in her hair.

Oh, shoot! Okay, not her best foot forward. "Cupcakes."

Linc briefly closed his eyes. "Dammit, I forgot. How much is there still to do?"

"A lot."

Cady, looking impatient, stepped between them and glanced at her watch. "Linc, we've got serious time constraints, and you're already fifteen minutes late. I need you changed and in the downstairs library in five minutes."

Linc dropped his laptop bag onto the hall table. "Dressed in jeans and a white button-down shirt?"

"Yes…casual, hip, no shoes," Cady quickly replied and, hearing the photographer shouting for her, she rushed down the hallway. Tate was about to turn away to head back downstairs to clean up the kitchen when Linc grabbed her wrist and tugged her to the stairs.

"Linc, Piper is cooking, and the kitchen looks like the world ended in there," Tate protested, yet her feet followed his hurried pace up the stairs.

"They can handle it," Linc replied. "Where's Shaw?"

"Downstairs, watching TV."

"Ellie?"

"Sage is changing her."

"So, you can spare me ten minutes?" he asked, as they hit the landing to the second floor.

"I suppose."

Linc led her down the hallway and reached past her to open the door to his bedroom, his hand on her back urging her inside. Tate's quick glance of the room registered brown and creams, a masculine space, but then Linc's arms were around her and his mouth was on hers, hot, deep, dark and breath-stealing sexy.

Oh, Lord, he could kiss, Tate thought dreamily. His mouth was assured and clever, his tongue silky, his breath sweet. Strong, muscular arms held her flush against his tall, hard frame, and Tate was grateful for his support because she was quite certain that every joint in her body was on the point of liquefying. Linc left one hand on her bottom, and the fingers of his other hand speared into her hair, gripping her head and, just like she'd imagined earlier, tilted it to allow his tongue deeper access into her mouth.

She could kiss Linc for years, eons, the rest of her life, Tate mused. When his big hand found her breast and his thumb drifted across her puckered nipple, she whimpered, groaned and whimpered again. Tate's hand caressed his back, his rib cage before both her hands came to rest on his lean hips, her stretched-out thumbs very close to his hard erection.

She wanted to unbuckle his belt, pull down the zipper, slide her hands into his underwear—

Linc pulled back to rest his forehead against hers. "I've thought about doing that, and more, all day. I've been less than useless."

"I burned the first batch of cupcakes because I was fantasizing about you," Tate admitted, her voice husky.

Linc's eyes gleamed with pleasure. "What was I doing?"

"This, pretty much," Tate whispered.

"This is pretty tame compared to what I've been imagining." Linc's big hand covered most of her cheek, and he placed his thumb in the center of her bottom lip. "I want you, Tate. Badly."

"I know. I want you, too," Tate confessed. "It's inconvenient and crazy, and there are a thousand reasons why it's a bad idea—"

"But you're going to let me take you to bed?"

She didn't have the strength or the willpower to walk away. This one time, she couldn't resist temptation. But, because she had to protect herself, she laid out the rules of engagement. That way, there couldn't be any misunderstandings.

"This is a very short-term arrangement, Linc. We're just two adults who are wickedly attracted to each other and who want nothing more than some no-strings-attached fun." She could do sex, she could do a fling. This couldn't be anything more, and he needed to know that. "This is temporary and an emotion-free zone. So, no expectations, okay?"

"Understood," Linc said. "Relax, Tate, I'm not asking for anything more. I'm not expecting anything from you but to share your body with me. No offense, but if I was looking for someone to settle down with, and I'm not, you're not what I'm looking for."

Dammit, why did she feel like he'd jabbed an ice pick into her heart? Stupid girl! "Because I am the least stable, traditional, least likely to stay at home, woman you know?"

Linc shrugged. "But you're, by far, the sexiest woman I've ever met, and I want you more than my next breath."

The fist clenching her heart relaxed, and Tate sent him a hesitant smile. She could do this; she'd separate sex from emotion and she would be fine. She had to be; anything else wasn't an option.

"And, last request, outside this room, we act normal," Tate insisted.

Linc smiled teasingly. "What's normal?"

She was trying to be serious, but Tate's mouth curved upward. "Fair point. But, to spell it out, I look after the kids and you...well, you do what you do."

"Doing you is high on my list," Linc growled.

Tate punched his shoulder, but her fist held all the impact of a puff of air. "Be serious. Do we have a deal?"

Linc grinned. "And I thought that I was a pushy negotiator." He laughed at her glare and held up his hands. "Peace. And, yes, we have a deal."

Linc replaced his hands on her hips and dropped his head to nuzzle his lips against her temple.

"Shall we seal it with another kiss?" Tate asked, surprised at her brazen words.

Linc looked tempted and then regretful. With a groan he stepped back and moved his hands from her waist to her hands. "Tate, if we go there again, we're going to get naked, very fast. And if I'm not downstairs soon, Cady will send Beck up to light a fire under me."

"We have such crap timing," Tate said, her tone mournful.

Linc laughed. "We really do." He glanced at his watch and sighed. "Our ten minutes are nearly up. Jeans and white shirt. What type of jeans? Which white shirt?"

Tate pulled her hands from his and walked into his spacious closet, sighing at the racks of suits, dress shirts on hangars in a myriad of colors and what seemed like a hundred ties.

"You have more clothes than I do," she stated, looking at his pile of jeans.

"Since you live out of a suitcase, most people do," Linc said, walking past her to flip through his selection of white shirts. His shoulder brushed hers, and he hauled in a breath and closed his eyes. "You smell divine, like chocolates and perfume. And vanilla."

"Chocolate and vanilla cupcakes," Tate replied, picking up a pair of designer jeans from a pile and discarding them. When she saw a pair of jeans with a rip in the knee and a very pale blue from too many wash cycles, she held them up. "These."

"I meant to throw those away," Linc said, looking doubtful. "They are seriously old. I wear them to— jeez, I never wear them anymore."

"They are perfect," Tate reassured him. "There is nothing sexier than a guy in a pair of ripped, well-worn, well-fitting jeans and a good shirt."

"If you say so." Linc pulled his tie from his neck, undid some shirt buttons and pulled his dress shirt out of the waistband of his suit pants. Gripping the back of his shirt by its collar, he yanked it over his head and dropped it to the floor. Tate stood, open-mouthed, taking in his broad chest softly dusted with hair, his mouthwateringly sexy six-pack and the bulging muscles in his arms.

She placed her hand on her stomach and softly whimpered. "Holy cupcakes with sprinkles on them."

Linc's head shot up, and his hand, about to unzip his pants, stilled. "Problem?"

Tate shook her head and met his eyes, allowing him to see the raw desire she knew was blazing there. "It's just you, I…" She waved her hand as if to fan herself. "So damn hot. I could jump you right now."

Linc scrubbed his hands over his face and swore. "I'm holding on by a thread here, Harper, and you're not helping."

"You're the one stripping!" Tate huffed.

Linc dropped a hard, quick, open-mouth kiss on her mouth. "God, you are so sexy, and I love the way you look at me."

Smiling coquettishly, she dragged her index finger down the middle of his chest and over the ridges his six-pack. "Very pretty, Ballantyne. I'm happy to taste as well as touch."

"*Shut up*, Harper. You're playing with fire," Linc muttered, unzipping his pants and pushing them down his hips. Tate dropped her gaze, and she saw the proof of his desire for her straining against the soft fabric of his underwear. Tate licked her lips and took a step toward him. Determined to have his mouth on hers, her hands on all that tanned, masculine, sexy skin.

Linc's hands on her shoulders stopped her in her tracks. "As much as I want your hands on me, I can't. Not now. So, do me a favor, please, honey?"

Honey? Lord, she'd never been called that, never heard the words from a deep-voiced guy with lust and need and appreciation in his eyes.

Anything. She'd do *anything* for him, but, man, she hoped the favor involved getting naked and up close and very, very personal. Tate cocked her head and begged her racing heart to slow down. "What?"

"Later tonight, I promise you I am going to make you scream, over and over again, from unrelenting pleasure."

Oh...gulp.

"But for now? Please, walk your seriously fantastic ass out of my bedroom and down the stairs. I need you to go so that things—" Linc gestured to his groin "—can settle down."

This was nuts, Tate thought. She'd never had such an intense, crazy, take-me-now-and-damn-the-consequences reaction to any man before. Why Linc? Why now? Why with the one man who was the embodiment of everything she'd never wanted? And why did she suspect that walking away from Linc—and she *would* because that was what she did—might end up breaking her heart?

She needed to back away, that was the clever thing to do. Get some distance, some air, try to settle down.

Tate nodded. Yes, walking away was the sensible choice. And she would. In a minute.

But before she did, she reached for a white dress shirt she'd seen earlier. It was plain white with black buttons, designer, expensive but interesting. She pulled it off the hanger and handed it to Linc. "Wear this, roll up the sleeves to the middle of your forearms. Don't wear that watch. Wear the one you had on the other day."

"The one with the black leather strap?" Linc asked. "It's vintage."

"It's seriously sexy. As are you." Tate dropped a quick kiss on his bare, big biceps. "And, Linc?"

"Yeah?"

"Remember to smile," she told him softly. "Your smile… It's dynamite."

Heat flared in Linc's smoky gray eyes. "I'll be down in…" He looked down at his erection and he groaned. "Give me five minutes. Then again, it's been a while… I might need ten."

It took all Linc's fortitude and willpower to sit through that interminable photo shoot, to take directions from Jose, the anal photographer. But a millennium later—okay, maybe ninety minutes later—Jose declared himself satisfied and Linc, wearing Connor's massive alexandrite ring on his middle finger, was finally released from hell, previously known as Connor's magnificent and lushly decorated library.

Needing a minute, Linc ducked into the bathroom, turned around and leaned his back against the door.

He turned Connor's ring on his middle finger, fascinated, as always, by its colors. When he'd stood by the windows of the library, the stone, in the natural light pouring in from the windows, had looked like a fine emerald, but now, under artificial light, it was the raspberry red of a fine Burmese ruby.

Connor had still been alive when he'd asked Kari to marry him, and thank God that he had been. Had he not, Linc might've been stupid enough to give Connor's ring to Kari on their engagement. She would've pawned it as she had her very expensive, stunning five-carat yellow diamond solitaire he'd handed over with his proposal. He could live with losing the diamond, but if he'd lost Connor's ring, he'd never forgive himself.

He still wanted to give it to his wife one day, if he ever found the one woman on whom he could take a chance. Linc pulled the ring off his finger and stared down at it as he imagined sliding the ring onto a feminine finger, looking tenderly into the eyes of the woman of his dreams. But instead of the blue or green eyes he normally conjured up, honey-brown eyes flashed on his mental big screen. Sparkling, warm, expressive eyes, a mobile mouth, tumbling, crazy blondish-brown hair.

Tate.

Linc shoved his ring back onto his finger and stood up to grip the edge of the tiny basin. He glared at his reflection in the mirror above the wall and told himself to get a clue.

Tate would never wear his ring because Tate was

not marriage material. Tate was a free spirit, someone who associated marriage and commitment with all the freedoms of jail.

Yes, they were wildly attracted to each other, and as soon as he could get rid of his family, as soon as the kids were asleep, he intended to discover every nook and cranny of that glorious body. He'd taste her, feed on her, but what he *wouldn't* do was get attached to her.

That way madness lay. Harper women didn't like restrictions or commitment. He'd learned his lesson with Kari and he'd learned it well. This time he'd be better prepared. This was about sex, pure and simple. Later tonight, he and Tate would light the match, set their attraction on fire and, like other chemical reactions, they would burn hard and fast, rocketing their way to a quick end.

Because they were on the same page and reading the same damn book, they'd be able to walk away from each other with only a couple of scorch marks and the wish that their spark could've burned longer and harder but understanding that intense reactions never lasted.

This was chemistry, nothing else. They hardly knew each other, were complete opposites and lived totally different lives. Chemistry was all they had…

Chemistry was all they *could* have, Linc reminded himself when a pang of longing coursed through his system. She was bold and mouthy and intense and complicated, for God's sake. She wasn't the quiet, stable, calm person he wanted.

She wasn't bland or boring, either, his inner devil told him, and Linc closed his eyes, frustrated at his turmoil. He hadn't felt this overwrought in years, not since…

Not since the other Harper woman dropped into his life and flipped it upside down.

Linc opened his eyes and ground his back teeth together. He would not allow Tate to upend his calm, controlled, orderly world. They'd have sex—there was no way he could deny himself that—but that was where their relationship started and ended.

In bed.

God, he couldn't wait to get that party started. Did the kids really need a bath? Shaw could, this once, miss out on his nightly story. There were a million places to eat in the city, his siblings could find food somewhere else…

He wanted, this one time, to put his needs and wishes first.

Eight

Linc jogged down the steps and stopped in the doorway to the kitchen and great room, taking in the chaos. A lasagna bubbled in the oven. Cady and Piper sat on the big leather couch closest to the kitchen, and Sage was in the chair opposite them, Ellie on her lap, holding her bottle and fighting sleep. Ty, Jaeger and Piper's son, sat in the high chair next to the granite-topped counter, and Shaw was perched on the counter itself, a piping bag of shocking green icing in his hand, biting his lip as he squeezed the contents onto a cupcake.

His burly brothers were standing on either side of Tate. Beck was using a small roller on what might or might not be bright yellow dough, and Jaeger was pressing a cookie cutter into garish purple icing.

These were going to be the brightest and messiest cupcakes in the history of pre-K bake days, Linc decided as he walked into the room.

Tate was the first to notice his arrival, and their eyes clashed and held as he walked across the great room. Judging by her glazed eyes and half-open mouth, she was reliving their X-rated, happened-in-the-closet kiss. He dragged his eyes off her before he embarrassed himself, and greeted Cady and Piper, bending down to drop a kiss on Sage's head. Because he could and she was cute, he kissed Ellie's head, as well. He walked over to the kitchen area and ran his hand over Shaw's bright head, taking a moment to connect with his son.

Shaw's eyes, that intense blue he shared with Kari, met his. "This is the best fun *ever*, Dad. We're making spacemen cupcakes."

Beck lifted his head and mock frowned at Shaw. "Spacemen? I thought we were making dinosaurs!"

"And I thought we were making monsters," Jaeger chimed in, joining the teasing.

"Spacemen," Shaw told them, his tone suggesting that they were both village idiots. He gestured to the badly decorated, messy batch of finished cupcakes, beaming with pride. Linc had never seen anything that looked less like spacemen in his life.

"They are so cool," Shaw said, his eyes sparkling with excitement.

"They really are, buddy," Linc lied, straight-faced. "How many do you still have to do?"

Shaw held up a half-decorated cupcake in his hand

and looked a little disgusted. "Just this one. Tate says that she has to make some that girls will eat, so she's going to do the rest later." Shaw sent Tate a hard look. "No pink and no fairies."

"But I can do flowers, right?" Tate asked, her mouth twitching.

"Just a few," Shaw reluctantly agreed.

Linc walked over to the huge fridge and pulled out three beers, opened two and placed them in front of his brothers. Unable to resist touching Tate, Linc allowed his fingers to slide up and under her shirt to find the band of soft skin just above the waistband of her leggings. "Wine, Tate?"

Linc noticed that Tate sucked in her breath as his fingers trailed over her skin. Oh, God, this waiting was killing both of them. Good to know that he wasn't alone in this madness.

"I'm good...thanks," Tate said as if she were battling to find her words.

Linc checked on the levels in the wineglasses across the room before twisting the cap off his beer bottle and taking a long sip. He was thirsty, hungry and tired but, mostly, he was horny. He'd ditch the beer and the food in a heartbeat if he could kiss that sexy spot where Tate's neck met her jawline...

"Have you made any progress finding out who is buying up Ballantyne stock?" Jaeger asked him, leaning his butt against the counter.

Linc, pulling his mind from the bedroom, shook his head. "No, not yet. But I will."

"As a family we own controlling shares, and as

long as we stick together, we are safe from a hostile takeover, so I don't seen the point of anyone buying up big blocks of stock. Combined, we own sixty percent of the company, but this company, Lach-Ty, now owns five percent. Worrying," Beck stated, picking up his beer.

Worrying about Ballantyne International was his job, as was protecting his family. But he'd done a crap job so far in regard to finding out who was behind the purchases of the shares. He had a company name, Lach-Ty, but little else. He loathed operating in the dark and decided to ask Reame to look into the situation. His pal had the skills, or employed people with the skills, to dig up the information he needed.

Linc placed a hand on his brother's shoulder. "I'll get to the bottom of it, Beck. It'll be okay, I promise."

"As long as we stand together," Beck replied, his tone giving away his concern.

"We always do. We always will," Jaeger told him, and Linc flashed him a grateful smile.

Jaeger nodded briefly. He glanced at the oven and bellowed, "Who is hungry?"

"Me!" Shaw shouted, waving the icing bag around. Linc saw splatters of radioactive green land on Tate's chin and chest. Reacting quickly, he reached across the counter and grabbed the bag from Shaw. "Easy, Shaw." He grinned at the streak of green in Tate's hair, the spots on her cheek. "Tate now looks like a spaceman."

Instead of rushing off to the bathroom in a panic to clean up, in order to look perfect, Tate dragged her finger across her chin and popped the icing she gathered into her mouth. Her gaze met Linc's, and his knees buckled at the lust and laughter in her eyes.

"At least I taste good." she murmured.

That he could vouch for...

"Well," Jaeger drawled, his eyes bouncing between them, "I have a feeling that dinner is going to be quick, and that big bro is going to be kicking us out of here as soon as we are done eating."

Linc didn't drop his eyes from Tate's.

"Damn straight," he muttered as Tate blushed. "Feel free to leave now. You can even take the lasagna with you."

Tate, feeling sticky and a little headachy from tension and anticipation, piped a pale yellow swirl onto a vanilla cupcake and reached for a premade bumblebee, carefully placing the little bee at an angle. Nine cupcakes down, three to go. Looking around the relatively clean kitchen, she couldn't help but smile. She'd been surprised, and grateful, when the Ballantyne brothers had cleaned up the mess they, and Shaw, had made in their effort to create their spacemen cupcakes. The dishwasher was loaded, the counters wiped down, the ingredients put away. Sage had even stayed to help her mix up four colored bowls of icing and had even offered to help decorate the next batch of cupcakes.

But Tate knew that Sage still had hours of work ahead of her, so she'd gently refused her help. Besides, she wanted to be alone with Linc. Well, as alone as they could get with two kids in the house. She just needed to get these last few cakes decorated, and she could take a shower and rid herself of her grimy jeans and sticky T-shirt. And then, God willing and children cooperating, Linc would blow her mind...

And, hopefully other parts of her body, as well.

Tate's head snapped up when she heard Linc's footsteps and sucked in her breath as he walked across the room to her. He stopped just behind her, slid his strong arms around her waist and laid his chin on her shoulder. "How many more to go?"

Tate tipped her head back to rest it against his collarbone, inhaling his masculine cologne and the underlying scent that was all Linc. "Three. It'll go quick, if I'm not distracted."

Linc nuzzled her temple before standing up straight. He dropped his arms and moved to stand next to her, his hip pushing into the counter. "What can I do to hurry this process along? I mean...to help?"

Tate lifted her eyebrows, trying not to laugh. "Are you any better at icing than your brothers and son?"

Linc smiled. "Not really." He gestured to her pretty cupcakes, a complete contrast to the other messy ones. "Yours look fantastic. Are you going to fix the spacemen?"

Tate shook her head. "I'm not going to do a thing."

"They aren't exactly of ChildTime standards," Linc said, and Tate heard the doubt in his voice.

"Screw the standard," Tate cheerfully told him. "Shaw made them, he loves them, that's all that matters. Besides, they are bright and sugary. The kids will inhale them."

Linc pushed his fingers into his short hair. "You're right. What Shaw thinks is all that's important." He walked over to the cupboard, pulled down two tumblers and a bottle of really expensive whiskey. Linc placed a half-full glass close to her, and she murmured her thanks.

"How was the photo shoot?" Tate asked, trying to think of something to talk about to keep both their minds off the smoking hot sex they were about to have.

She also needed a distraction from the realization that she'd loved everything about this evening, had so relished feeling like an integral part of a family, like she was needed and important. Normally, she would've avoided anything that smacked of Harriet Homemaker and run at the first hint of domesticity, but she'd thoroughly enjoyed herself. She even—dare she think it?—wanted more.

You're losing your mind, Harper. You're just over-excited because you're about to get laid, and your brain is working overtime.

Get a grip.

"Long," Linc replied, boosting himself up to sit on the counter next to her work space. God, how was she supposed to concentrate on her swirls when his long, muscled thigh was a few inches from her hand, when she could see his tanned flesh through the rips in his jeans?

Tate noticed the unusual ring on his middle finger. "Jaeger had Kashmir sapphires. Beck, red beryl. Sage, red diamonds, but I don't recognize your stone."

"Alexandrite." Linc pulled the ring off his finger and held it between his thumb and forefinger. He turned it, and in the red depths Tate caught a flash of green, then yellow, maybe a hint of orange. It was stunningly beautiful.

"Emerald by day, ruby by night," Linc explained. "It changes color depending on the light source."

"I've never seen you with it before." Tate picked up the bag of yellow icing and pulled a bare cupcake toward her.

"Despite my job, I'm not a jewelry-wearing type of guy. This was Connor's ring. I was with him, the day he discovered this stone," Linc explained, his voice low.

Beneath the lust hovering between them, she heard nostalgia and longing in his voice as he shared an incredible memory. Yes, of course she wanted to explore his fabulous body, but she didn't mind taking a stroll through his amazing mind. "Tell me more."

"It was about six months after we moved in here, and I was recovering from chicken pox. I was better, but the doctor insisted that I stay home, and I was bored out of my mind. I couldn't believe it when Connor invited me to attend an estate sale with him, somewhere upstate. He bid and won this box of what was mostly costume jewelry. But amongst the junk was a stunning ruby pendant and this ring. Connor was beside himself, alexandrite was his favorite stone, and the ring slid onto his finger as if it were made for him. He never took it off until the day he died."

"And you inherited it."

Linc's big shoulders rose and fell. "He was my

dad, the only dad I knew. Or wanted. He never married, but, with my mom's help, he raised four kids and made us feel loved every damn day."

"And he and your mom?"

Linc smiled. "They were best friends, and she was devastated when he died, but nothing, as far as I knew, sparked between them."

"And she had no problem with him adopting you?"

Linc shrugged. "I think she did in the beginning. But they worked it out. He wanted me as much as he wanted the others, and I was his son, with or without her permission. Connor convinced her that him becoming my dad didn't stop her from being my mom."

Tate placed her hand on his knee and squeezed. "You must miss him."

"So damn much. He was my North Star, my magnetic pole. Funny, so smart, so full of life. He was, in so many ways, the glue that held us together. He was our charismatic, fearless leader."

"And now you've taken over that role," Tate observed, thinking how much responsibility Linc carried on his big, broad shoulders.

"Yeah, I suppose," Linc replied, his voice scratchy with emotion.

"And are you okay with doing that?"

"Connor would expect it, and that's reason enough. Though, admittedly, there are days when I'd like to run away." Linc lifted his glass to his lips, and Tate noticed the slight tremble in his fingers. "While this family mostly, runs on discussion and democracy,

the buck has to stop with someone, and that someone is me."

"Your siblings would probably disagree with that.
And, to be honest, they look like they are very capable of running their own lives."

"They are," Linc admitted. "And they do, but they
all know that I'm standing behind them, ready to
catch them if they fall. As for the company, I'll protect
the Ballantyne wealth and assets with my last breath."

He would, Tate realized. His son, his family and
their loved ones, were at the center of everything
Linc did. He existed to protect his family and the
company his father had loved and created. But where
did that leave his wants and desires? He was so busy
giving that he rarely took, probably didn't think that
he had the right to be loved and protected and cher-
ished himself.

*I could, if I was braver, less independent and not
terrified of staying in one place, I could love him. I
could give him what he needed.*

But, realistically, all she could give him was sex.
Hot, intense, hopefully mind-blowing sex. Sex that
he wouldn't forget.

Tate reached for a pink rose, plunked it on top of
the last swirl of icing and ignored the last bare cupcake. She tossed the piping bag on the counter and
pushed her hair off her forehead with the back of
her wrist.

She was done. She wanted a shower and this man.
Now.

Tate looked at Linc. "Shaw asleep?"

He nodded.

Tate gestured to the baby monitor. "So is Ellie."

Linc, not moving a muscle, just looked at her, his eyes blazing. Oh, God, was she going to have to spell it out for him? Maybe she could write *Let's Strip* on the counter with pale pink icing. Tate held her breath as Linc dropped to his feet to stand so close to her that her breasts brushed his chest. He picked up a strand of her hair and twirled it between his fingers. She sighed when she saw the green icing from her hair now smeared on his fingers. "You're a mess, Harper."

She agreed. "I know. I'll go shower and—"

"You're a hot, sexy mess," Linc murmured, ignoring her interruption. "You smell of sugar and chocolate and some perfume that drives me insane. You aren't wearing a shred of makeup, yet your face looks like it should be on the cover of a fashion magazine."

Linc placed his hand on her cheek, and his thumb drifted across her cheekbone. Tate gripped his strong wrist as his sexy words flowed over her, into her, heating her blood and drying up the moisture in her mouth.

Linc's thumb moved to her mouth. "I can't wait to touch you, taste you, to see you naked. I know that my fantasies will not match the reality."

Tate placed her hands on his chest and sucked in a deep breath. "All I need is a quick shower," she begged.

Linc bent his knees and in one fluid, easy movement, scooped her into his arms. Tate wrapped her arm around his neck, as she absorbed the heat from

his hard, lean body. "You can shower later, sweetheart, preferably with me. I've waited too long for
you. I'm not waiting any longer."

"But—"

Linc ignored her protest and strode over to the
couch, holding her close to him before allowing her
feet to drift to the floor. "I need you, Tate. Now."

Since she sensed that Linc rarely, if ever, used *need*
and *you* in the same sentence, she just linked her arms
around his neck and stood on her tiptoes to brush
her mouth across his. She couldn't give him what he
needed, deserved, on a long-term basis, but she could
give him what he needed tonight. *That* she could do.

"I'm here, Linc. Take me."

Linc, smart man that he was, didn't need any further encouragement, and he quickly pulled her shirt
up and over her head. Dropping the sticky garment
to the floor, Tate watched his face as he looked down
at her chest, his hands moving to cup her breasts in
his big, masculine hands.

"So pretty, Tate."

To Tate's surprise, Linc lifted his hands from her
breasts to tunnel his fingers into her heavy mass of
hair, and he angled her face to receive his no-holds-
barred kiss. Tongues tangoed as he devoured her
mouth, learning her taste, her essence, silently telling her that he wanted more.

That he wanted all that she had.

Exhilarated by his passion and his low, guttural
murmurs of appreciation, Tate undid the buttons of
his shirt and pushed it open so that she could explore

the hot skin of his wide chest, to discover the hard muscles underneath.

So sexy, she thought, pure masculine strength. Tate's fingers traced the ridges of his stomach and moved on to the long muscles on either side of his hips and couldn't resist the urge to dance her fingers across the powerful erection that tented his jeans.

Oh, yeah. He felt amazing, and, judging by Linc's sudden gasp, he liked what she was doing as much as she did. And she liked it a *lot*. Teasing him, Tate traced his long length with the tip of her finger.

"Tate."

He muttered her name against her mouth, but she heard the desire and the demand in his voice. Linc's hands skated down her back to find her bra strap which he snapped open with a minimum of fuss. The cups of her lace bra fell away, and Linc pulled the fabric off her bare breasts, revealing her hard, pink nipples to his gaze.

"Yeah, so damn pretty," Linc breathed as his hands moved to the waistband of her leggings, pushing the fabric down her hips to reveal her tiny panties to his hot, hungry gaze.

His hands gripped and released her hips as he looked down at her, past her flat stomach, over the neat landing strip showing through the transparent fabric to her long legs.

"You are sheer perfection."

She wasn't, but she appreciated the words.

"You're not too bad yourself, Ballantyne," Tate

whispered, dropping a wet, open-mouth kiss on his bare chest as she attempted to undo his belt buckle.

Linc slid his hand between her legs and cupped her, his thumb immediately finding and brushing her sensitive spot through the fabric of her thong, causing her to moan into his chest. If she didn't get her hands on him soon...

"Help me, Linc. I need to feel you," Tate told him, looking up as she laid her flat palm on him, wishing that she had a spell to magically make clothes evaporate.

Linc's hand pressed hers against his erection, and she heard his ragged breathing, his low curses.

"We need to slow this down. If we don't, I'm going to toss you onto that couch and take you, right here, right now."

And that would be a problem? "Since that's exactly what I want—hot, fast, furious—I'm wondering why you are waiting."

Linc reached behind him and pulled out a strip of three condoms from the back pocket of his jeans. He ripped off a packet with his teeth and allowed the rest to fall to the floor. He dropped the packet into her hand with a wicked, tempting smile. "You said that you want to get your hands on me," he teased.

"If you helped me with your pants, I would," Tate retorted, opening the foil packet.

Linc lifted an amused eyebrow. "Feeling flustered, sweetheart?"

Tate looked him in the eye. "Aren't you? We have

all this raging heat, and I can't wait to stand in the ring of fire and burn with you."

Linc undid his belt and, using just one hand, flipped open the buttons to his jeans. He pushed his jeans and underwear down his hips, and Tate caught her breath when she saw his big erection standing straight and proud.

She flashed him a grin. "Wow. Talking about pretty..."

Linc groaned when her small hand encircled him, and nipped her jaw with his teeth. "*Pretty?* Try another, more manly adjective please?" he teased, laughter in his voice.

"Impressive? Masculine? Bold?" Tate rubbed her thumb lightly over the head of his shaft.

"Those will work," Linc growled, pushing her thong over her hips. When they were completely naked, he sat down on the couch and pulled Tate onto him, so that her knees straddled his thighs.

As his hands moved between her legs she curled her hand around his long and thick erection. She didn't want to wait. She wanted to be pushed, possessed, filled, taken to the limit. She wanted to feel as if she like belonged here, with him, just for this brief slice of time.

As Linc tested her readiness by sliding his finger into her, Tate pulled out the condom and swiftly rolled it over him, sucking in her breath as he hardened even more.

"Tate, I don't think I can wait any longer. I need to be inside you," Linc said, his voice rough with need. "I know it's our first time, and I should be taking it

slow but…dammit, I don't think I can." Not giving
her time to reply, Linc hooked his big hands under
her thighs and lifted her up, spreading her legs so that
the head of his shaft probed her wet, feminine core.
Linc's hands on her hips gently guided her down as
he thrust into her with one long, confident stroke.
Tate felt herself liquefying, her entire focus on how
Linc felt inside her. Her vision tunneled and there was
just the two of them in the world, and making love
was all that was important, all that could ever matter. Linc's hands on her skin, his mouth under hers,
him filling those long neglected spaces was all she
could focus on.

Linc held her breasts in his hands, his fingers ca-
ressing her ultrasensitive nipples, and his tongue in
her mouth mimicked the thrust of his hips, the sure
strokes as he lifted her closer to the sun.

"Come for me, honey, let me feel you," Linc
coaxed, his forehead against hers.

Tate was beyond speech, so she replied by grinding down on him as lightning danced along her skin.

Linc moved his head so that he could speak directly in her ear. "You feel so good. So sexy. Take
me, Tate, take all of me. Yeah, like that."

Her mind and body full of him, Tate reached for
her release, and she shouted as another bolt of lightning skittered through her and splintered her body
into a million pieces. Somewhere, from a place far
away, she heard Linc's demands in her ear, his words
not making sense. But his body did, and she understood the silent demand that she reach for more. She

wanted to tell him that she couldn't, that it was all too much, but then he touched a place deep inside her and she exploded again, harder and faster than before.

A century might've passed, or maybe it was only a minute or two, before she came back to herself, her cheek against his chest, his arms holding her tight.

"We did it," Linc murmured, his hand brushing her hair off her cheek.

"We most certainly did," Tate agreed, her mouth curving into a satisfied smile.

"The sex was fantastic, I agree, but I was referring to the fact that we managed to make love without one of the kids waking up."

Oh, right. She'd forgotten about the kids upstairs. But until one of them yelled, she wasn't moving a muscle. "Yay."

"Want to see if we can do it again while the going is good?" She heard Linc's smile in his words, felt the curve of his lips against her bare shoulder.

Tate nodded. Nobody could ever accuse her of not being up for the challenge.

"Slow and sexy this time?" Tate asked.

Linc's wonderful mouth curved upward. "Sexy every time, sweetheart."

Nine

Tate, always slow to wake up, pulled a strand of hair out of her mouth and groaned into her pillow. Fighting the urge to slide back into sleep, she yawned, frowning when she realized the pillowcase was a deep chocolate color and not the snowy white fabric she normally woke up to.

Linc. Sex. All night long. They'd started on the couch and ended in his bedroom. Twice, three times, four if you counted the heavy petting they'd shared in the shower. They'd been insatiable, turning to each other time and again, consumed by the need to give and receive pleasure.

He was the best lover she'd ever had... Admittedly, she hadn't had that many men in her bed, but she was convinced that if she had, he'd still be the best. Tender, demanding and confident and, surprisingly, uninhibited, Linc seemed to shed his calm, reserved, everything-can-be-worked-out attitude with his clothes and morphed into a dirty-talking, demanding, unrestrained lover.

Tate had no complaints. Nope, she couldn't think of one. Well, maybe a little one: she was in his bed and he wasn't touching her. That, she decided, could be easily remedied. Tate rolled over, and instead of encountering Linc's hot, hard, naked warmth, her hand landed on a small body wearing flannel pajamas covered in helicopters. Tate immediately glanced down at her chest and sighed her relief when she realized that she was wearing one of Linc's T-shirts.

Thoroughly confused, she lifted her head to look over Shaw's sprawled-out body and saw Ellie lying on Linc's T-shirt-covered chest, her face tucked into his neck and his hand covering her small back. His eyelashes were spikes against his cheeks, and heavy stubble covered his jawline.

Tate noticed the baby monitor on the bedside table next to him and tried to make sense of the time between falling asleep naked and now. She'd acquired a shirt, Linc had pulled on some clothes, and the huge bed they'd made love in had been invaded by two little people.

They looked like a family, Tate thought, panic creeping up her throat. This was what she'd had as a kid, two parents, lazy Saturday morning sleep-ins.

"Welcome to life with kids," Linc drawled, his growly voice dancing over her skin.

Tate pushed her elbow into the bed and rested her head in her hand. She looked across Shaw to Linc, who had yet to open his eyes. "When did they wake up?"

Linc cracked open one eye and lifted his wrist to look at his high-tech watch. "Shaw wandered in at about five, Miss Ellie was bellowing at six."

Tate winced. "I didn't hear a thing. You should've roused me."

Linc rolled his head and his smoky eyes met hers. Heat curled through her at the appreciation in his gaze. "I tried. You didn't even stir when I poured you into my shirt."

"That might be because we only got to sleep a few hours ago." She gestured to Ellie. "But thanks. I owe you."

"You do," Linc replied, his smile lazy. "If we were alone, I'd show you how you could repay me."

Tate blushed, thinking of how well he'd loved her. She opened her mouth to make a witty retort, but her brain had nothing. Zip. Not because Linc was six feet something of pure, primal male but because she'd rolled back in time. Remembering the little girl she'd been, climbing into her parents' bed at the crack of dawn, waking up in her dad's arms, her face tucked into his neck, hearing his whiskey-rough voice telling her to go back to sleep.

She'd had a few years of happiness and security, but that had been ripped away when Kari and Lauren dropped into their house and lives. Nothing lasted forever, and as sweet and wholesome as this little scenario was, her past reminded her that it wasn't hers to keep. Sex was one thing, but playing happy family with Linc and these gorgeous children was not something she could indulge in. She might come to like it and, worse, come to yearn for it. She'd lost one family unit; she wasn't going to set herself up to lose another.

Tate was about to sit up when Ellie's eyes slowly opened and focused on her face. She yawned and lifted her little hand in Tate's direction, her extraordinary blue eyes full of love. Smiling, she crawled off Linc's chest, over the still-sleeping Shaw and into Tate's arms. Ah, dammit, Tate thought as Ellie's chubby arms wound around her neck and the little girl burrowed closer, her nose under Tate's jaw, her hands tangled in her long hair.

This was trust at its purest form, Tate thought, holding Ellie tight and closing her eyes, feeling the wash of love breaking over her, holding all the pent-up power of the sea. Oh, God, she couldn't fall in love with Ellie, couldn't start thinking of being her family, her primary caregiver, of making a family with her.

How was she supposed to look after a little girl with the type of career she had? Babies and border posts were not a happy combination at the best of times, and taking Ellie with her would be utterly impractical.

Keeping Ellie with her would mean sacrificing her career—a career that earned her a lot of money and that she loved. With Ellie in her arms, Tate stood up and walked over to the window of Linc's bedroom, pushing aside the heavy drapes to look down at the icy road below. She released a heavy sigh. If she even dared to imagine giving up her freedom and her independence to raise Ellie, how would she support them? She had a healthy bank account and she could probably buy an apartment—not in Manhattan obviously—and ensure that they had a roof over their heads. But she'd still have to feed them, clothe them, pay the utilities, and to do that she'd need a job. A job, in this context, meant staying in one place, and Tate shuddered. She hadn't had a fixed abode in years, and she didn't think she could do it.

A bigger worry was that Ellie was starting to attach to her, as she'd just shown by leaving Linc's arms to crawl to her. Would she psychologically damage her niece when she gave her back to her mom? How would being a human equivalent of pass-the-parcel affect Ellie long-term? Would she have trust issues? Tate wouldn't blame her if she did.

Tate felt Linc's hands on her waist and sighed when his big body pressed up against hers, her back to his chest, his chin resting on the top of his head. "Is this all feeling a bit too real?" he asked, his deep voice gentle.

Tate nodded, a ball constricting her throat. "I don't think I can do this, Linc."

She had to pull back, she had to find that place of inner solitude that served her so well. She had to retreat to her mental island where emotions couldn't affect her.

"Do what, Tate? Us?"

"No, that I can do because I know it's just sex."

Not understanding the reason for Linc's sudden tension, she ignored it.

"I'm not sure I can be what Ellie needs," Tate said, her voice cracking. "She's starting to trust me, starting to rely on me, but in a couple of days, or in a few weeks, I'm going to hand her back to Kari—"

"If you find her."

"Reame will find her," Tate stated. He had to; she couldn't imagine having to make the final and crucial decisions about Ellie's future. That was Kari's job, dammit. "I'm worried that I will end up hurting her by loving her, by bonding with her knowing that that bond will be severed soon."

Linc rubbed his chin over her hair, and Tate felt the reassuring squeeze on her hips. "Tate, trust is a learned skill. When we teach children to love and to trust by being loving and trustworthy, they learn that they can expect that from other adults."

Tate snorted her disbelief. "Can't see Kari teaching Ellie those life lessons."

"Me, neither." Linc released her to stand beside her, leaning his shoulder into the wall, his face solemn. "I accept that you are worried about Ellie's well-being, but I suspect that you are also worried about your emotions, your state of mind."

Tate rubbed Ellie's back with her hand, realizing that the little girl had fallen back to sleep. She tipped her head to the side, not sure if she wanted to hear what Linc was about to say.

"You don't like the emotions and you're worried for yourself, worried that you are becoming too attached to her. You're worried that you will be hurt when she moves on."

Oh, damn, she really was. She didn't want to miss Ellie, or Shaw, didn't want to miss Linc. She *so* didn't want to miss Linc. And she would. She'd spent so little time with him, but this house, this stupidly big mansion had become a place she loved, and the people who lived inside it, and who were associated with it, people she had come to truly like. Leaving The Den would hurt like hell.

"The thing is, getting too attached is exactly what Ellie needs from you even though it might break your heart one day. Because showing her love and affection is the right thing to do. She's the innocent party here, Tate. She didn't choose a damn thing, so if you withhold love and affection, you'd be punishing her for something she didn't create." Linc lifted his hand to clasp the back of her neck, dropping his head to rest his forehead on hers. "The only thing you can do is to make it as easy on her as possible. Even if that might make life harder for yourself."

"This isn't me, Linc!" Tate cried. "I don't want this responsibility. I want to be free and independent and only want to be responsible for myself."

"That's the easy route, sweetheart," Linc said, his voice low and rough. "Having no ties, no commitments, no responsibility is an easy—possibly lonely—way to live. You only have to think about yourself, all the time. It's a way to protect yourself from life and from all the crap it throws at you. And it's a really good way to avoid getting hurt."

He was right, of course he was. His words felt like hailstones smacking her soul, but he was speaking the truth, and she appreciated his honesty.

"Why the traveling, Tate? Why do you keep running from place to place?" Linc gestured for her to sit down on the large wing chair next to the bed, and Tate lowered herself and Ellie to the chair, grateful to get off her wobbly legs. She stared out of the window, watching cold raindrops slide down the windows.

Linc sat down on the edge of the bed, his knee nudging hers, his forearms on his thighs, his expression intense. "Talk to me, Tate. God knows you need to talk to someone."

Ellie, disturbed by her aunt's movements, sat up, rubbed her eyes and spat out her pacifier. She pushed Tate's hands off her, crawled off her lap and dropped her feet to the floor, one hand holding the chair and the other holding Linc's leg for balance. She wobbled before plopping down onto her butt. Smiling, she started to crawl away. Tate reached for her, but Linc's hand on her bare knee stopped her. "She's fine, Tate, let her crawl. Talk to me."

Tate knew that if she told Linc that she didn't want to talk about her past, he would respect her wishes, but she wanted him to know the forces that shaped her into the person she was. Keeping it simple and brief, she reminded him about her childhood, her parent's divorce, her mother's preference for her niece and why she and her sister didn't speak for years.

"Thanks for defending me—us." Linc said.

"My fight with Kari, about her leaving you and

Shaw the way you did, caused an additional strain between my mother and me. We didn't speak much after that. Then she died and our relationship could never be repaired."

"I'm sorry, honey."

Tate crossed her legs and turned, resting her head against the back of the chair. "I'm sorry that two more Harper women have turned your life upside down again."

Linc's eyes gleamed with amusement. "That's okay...last night was worth any aggravation."

She needed to say it, needed to express another apology. "I'm especially sorry that Kari's actions caused you to shy away from love and relationships, Linc. You've given her too much power. Not all women are like that. You should try again. You're a good guy, and you deserve to be happy."

Linc kept his eyes pinned to hers, and she saw the flash of annoyance in those granite depths. "Pot calling the kettle black, Tate? Her actions have dictated the course of your life, too. You're the one who has run from commitments and people and stability because your family pushed you aside. Are you brave enough to change that?"

"No, I don't think so."

Linc released a long, slow breath before standing up. "Yeah. Me, neither." He ran his hands over his head, his shirt inching up his stomach to reveal the dark trail wandering down from his six-pack abs. "I'm going downstairs to make coffee. Want me to take Ellie with me so that you can grab a shower?"

Discussion over, Tate thought with relief. She nodded her thanks and watched as Linc scooped up Ellie and held her like a football, Ellie laughing in delight.

He looked down at her and then back at Tate, his gaze suddenly serious. "The trick is to enjoy them, Tate, for as long as you have them."

He was talking about Ellie but also about them, about the night they shared. He was right—she should just live each moment and deal with whatever life threw at her when she could see it barreling her way.

No promises and no guarantees. Especially from him. *Got it, Ballantyne.*

A week passed and it was another cold Saturday afternoon, and Tate had The Den to herself. Linc had taken Shaw to a birthday party and wasn't expected to be back until the early evening. Ellie had fallen asleep in the middle of Tate's bed after lunch, so after transferring her to the crib, Tate went downstairs, feeling a little at a loss. She hadn't spent much time on her own for more than three weeks, so how was she going to fill the next couple of hours?

She supposed she could work out. Linc had told her to make use of his gym in the basement, but the last thing she felt like doing was spending her alone time sweating. She could watch some TV, but that didn't appeal. A movie? Tate wrinkled her nose...

What she really wanted to do was to climb into bed with Linc and spend a lazy afternoon enjoying that delicious, masculine body. At the bottom of the stairs, Tate halted, her hand on the newel post. God, she was seriously addicted to Linc, her mind constantly occupied with thoughts of him, in bed and out.

Tate plopped her butt onto the bottom stair and placed her chin her hands, her elbows on her knees. She wasn't acting anything like the nanny she was supposed to be.

Oh, she collected Shaw from school, entertained him in the afternoons allowing Linc to put in a solid day at work. When he came home she didn't, like a good nanny, walk up the stairs and retreat to her own quarters. Nope, instead she ran straight into his arms. Sometimes, depending on what the kids were doing, they hustled up the stairs, taking a few minutes to rocket each other to a body-blasting orgasm, something to take the edge off until they fell into bed later.

She missed work, of course she did, but not as much as she had expected to. For someone who liked being alone, who felt itchy when she was pinned to a spot for too long, she was remarkably content. And that scared the pants off her. And when she imagined going back to work, to returning to her life of airports and customs control, impersonal hotels and tourist traps, to living life on her own, her heart rebelled. She couldn't imagine giving up her job, relinquishing her independence and her freedom—she loved what she did far too much—but the notion of giving up Linc and the kids threw her into a tailspin. She didn't want to live a life without them in it. And deep down in her heart she knew why.

She'd kind of, sort of, fallen a little bit in love with

The Den, with the Upper East Side, with being Ellie's mommy and Shaw's nanny.

It was also very possible that she was in love with her sister's ex.

Oh, crap!

Tate dropped her head between her bent knees and sucked in a choppy breath. *Say it isn't so!*

No, no, no, Tate.

No! You weren't supposed to fall in love with him, you idiot. This was about sex, about a mutual fling; it wasn't supposed to get this intense this quickly.

Tate cursed herself, thinking that she'd definitely forgotten to pay her brain bill.

She couldn't be in love, she *wouldn't* be, Tate decided. She'd just been temporarily seduced by this lovely house and two cute kids and a man who made her catch her breath every time he walked into the room. She was just reliving the last time she'd been part of a family, and she was projecting that happiness onto the here and now.

Reality check, Harper. Reame was going to call, someday soon, and tell her that he'd found Kari, and then she'd return Ellie to her mom's not-so-loving arms. Man, that would bite. Then, because she had nothing to keep her in the city—she and Linc were as temporary as a social media trend—she'd move out of The Den, and maybe they'd see each other now and again until her vacation was over. She'd receive her next assignment, start working on a new series and she'd be sent God knew where.

She could never risk loving Linc, creating a family

with him within the greater Ballantyne clan and then, like before, having it all ripped away. She wouldn't survive losing another family, losing the people she loved again. Linc and Ellie and Shaw could only be a lovely memory.

That was the way it had to be, the way it would be, so why was her stomach churning and bile creeping up her throat at the thought? Why did the notion of getting on a plane and leaving them behind make her feel like she was facing her executioner? *You're losing it, Harper, so get off your butt and do something! Call Reame, find out what progress he's made with finding Kari. Contact your producer and see if they have decided where they are sending you next.*

Get real. Stop fantasizing about something you can't have, and let these crazy notions about loving Linc, having it all, go. You have to move on.

Mentally and, sometime soon, physically.

But for now, step off the crazy train, dammit. She pinched the bridge of her nose and sighed. Maybe exercising wasn't a bad idea after all; maybe she could sweat out her stupidity.

Ten

Linc stood in front of the glass case holding Connor's alexandrite ring, a glass of whiskey in his hand. Around him, the rich and elite of Manhattan, and a few dozen other cities, drank French champagne and popped dainty canapés into mouths filled with perfect teeth.

Sage's edgy, interesting, modern collection was a roaring success, and the Ballantyne collection of rare precious gemstones was going to be talked about for a long time to come. Amy had volunteered to babysit Shaw and Ellie, and when he'd checked in with her ten minutes ago, both kids were asleep.

For the first time in, well, ages, he was having fun, and that was only because Tate was with him, sharing her pithy observations about his guests. She looked exquisite in a deep red lace dress. The high-waisted bodice was accented with a rose-printed lace, velvet strips and crystals. She'd found the dress in a vintage shop in SoHo, she'd told him, but Linc was more interested in the slight swell of her breasts peeking out from the neckline, her creamy shoulders and the smooth leg the thigh-high slit in the dress occasionally revealed.

She was beautiful, Linc thought, looking across the room to where Tate stood, talking to a tall, black-haired man who had his back to him. The man turned, and Linc saw his distinctive profile... Tyce Latimore, Sage's ex. Linc looked around the room to find his sister and saw her by the bar, talking to Reame. He'd once hoped that something would spark between Reame and Sage, but it never had; Reame treated Sage like a sister.

Linc turned his attention back to Tate and narrowed his eyes when Latimore placed his hand on Tate's back to guide her to the bar. His protective instincts revving in the red zone—there was vibe to Latimore that made Linc think that there was something unbridled and dangerous lurking beneath the smooth veneer—Linc pushed his way through the crowd to reach the bar. Sage, seeing Latimore's approach, slid off her seat and sauntered away, her ex's gaze following her, his expression benign but his eyes blazing. When he reached the bar, Linc pulled Tate to his side and gave Latimore a hands-off-or-I'll-beat-the-crap-out-of-you look.

Latimore just lifted a dark eyebrow and smiled

sardonically before holding out his hand for Linc to shake.

Linc shook his hand but deliberately kept a frown on his face. "Are you messing with my sister, Latimore?"

"Since she's currently not talking to me, and hasn't for a couple of months, that's not a feasible assumption," Tyce replied, his voice deep and dark. Linc thought he saw sadness flash in his eyes but dismissed the thought; the Korean French American was far too much of a player to be fazed that his sister was ignoring him.

"My warning still stands. You hurt Sage again and the three of us will take you apart." Linc pushed the words out through gritted teeth.

Linc heard and ignored Tate's surprised gasp. Tyce held his stare but banged his whiskey glass on the counter of the bar, and when he spoke, his words were bitter. "Yeah, you Ballantynes are such freakin' paragons. Have you ever considered that she might have hurt me, that one of yours might have hurt one of mine? You don't have the monopoly on family and loyalty, Ballantyne."

Latimore released a muttered curse and held his hand up. "Forget I said that." He fixed a smile onto his face, but Linc noticed that it didn't reach his deep brown, almost-black eyes. "It's been lovely meeting you, Tate. I hope we do so again."

"Not damn likely," Linc muttered.

Latimore flashed him a disparaging smile before Tyce's attention was caught by movement at the door.

Linc followed his gaze and saw his sister, in a midnight blue ball gown, taking a glass of champagne from a passing waiter's tray. As if she knew that Tyce was looking at her, she lifted her head, and their eyes clashed and held. Linc's eyes bounced from his sister to Latimore and back again, slightly uncomfortable at seeing the blazing attraction and undisguised lust on Sage's face.

Oh, God, she looked at Latimore like he did at Tate, like the thrill of riding the lightning bolt was worth ending up as a charred crisp.

"Holy smokes," Tate breathed, lifting her hand to fan her face. "That's some intense sexual attraction."

Linc signaled to the bartender for another glass of whiskey before frowning down at Tate. "Please do not mention sexual attraction and my sister in the same sentence," he growled.

"She's all grown-up." Tate pointed out the obvious, and his frown deepened.

"Not helping, honey." Linc nodded his thanks at the bartender and took a fortifying sip of his drink. Staring down into the liquid that was the same color as Tate's eyes, he shook his head. "God, that's going to end badly."

"Tyce and Sage?" Tate clarified.

"Yeah. I'd hoped they were over, but any fool can see that they aren't done with each other. And what did he mean by that your-family-hurting-mine comment?"

"A business deal that went south? A party invitation that wasn't sent? His grandmother had an affair with your grandfather?"

Linc rolled his eyes. "You're letting your imagination run away with you. No, Latimore doesn't come from family money. He's got to where he is by his own hard work."

"And you admire that."

"I do," Linc reluctantly admitted. "And I worry about the fact that Sage is so much wealthier than him."

Tate tipped her head to the side. "Does it bother you that you are so much wealthier than I am?" she asked him.

"No, that doesn't mean a damn thing," Linc said brusquely, wondering if he should feel insulted.

"Then why do you assume that it's a problem for him?" Tate asked. "The reality is that most men would be less wealthy than your sister. She could probably buy a small third-world country."

Linc smiled, acknowledging her point. "Only a small one, she wouldn't be greedy," he replied, only half joking.

"For what it's worth, I like him," Tate stated, crossing one leg over the other and revealing a very silky thigh. It took Linc thirty seconds to get his head out of the bedroom and to register Tate's words.

Jealousy, acid and unwelcome, flared. "You and the rest of the female population of the city," he groused. "He's said to be one of the best-looking and most talented bachelors in Manhattan."

"He is a fabulous artist," Tate agreed. "His sculptures are amazing."

"That's not the talent I was referring to," Linc said, his voice desert dry.

Instead of blushing, Tate erupted into laughter. When she could speak, she looked at him with mirth-filled eyes. "Oh, lucky, lucky Sage."

"Dammit, Tate!" Linc muttered, scowling into his drink.

Seeing his ferocious expression, her mouth quirked with amusement, and she lifted her hand in a placating gesture. Funny, he wasn't placated.

"His, um, talents aside, Tyce is a very good-looking man. He has a blinding smile, and his mixed heritage has resulted in a very, very sexy face. His body isn't too bad, either."

Linc groaned. "God, shoot me now."

"But he has sad eyes, and behind the charm and the charisma, I sense a man who hasn't had it easy. He has demons nipping at his heels," Tate stated, her tone now serious.

Linc wanted to believe that Latimore had all the depth of a puddle, so he wasn't happy with her pronouncement. Then again, nothing about this conversation made him happy. Especially Tate's comments on how attractive she found his sister's ex. "And you can tell this, how?"

Tate sipped her champagne. "Call it woman's intuition."

God, he hated those airy explanations, those inexplicable feelings women got that allowed them to make major assumptions on minimal information. But the hell of it was that he couldn't discount her pronouncement. Still, where Tate saw sadness, he saw danger, and he was worried that Sage was part of whatever game Tyce was playing.

Because Tyce Latimore, he was convinced, was playing a very dangerous game with someone.

Reame's hand gripping his shoulder pulled Linc out of his reverie. He sent his friend a weary smile, and when Reame's eyes remained serious, Linc frowned. Oh, crap. Something had happened. Something he didn't want to hear.

"Can you leave?" Reame asked Linc. He gestured to Beck and Cady, who were cheek to cheek on the dance floor. "I know that we are celebrating Beck's engagement, but we need to talk."

Linc slapped his glass on the counter and nodded. Tate put a hand on Linc's arm to hold him in place. "Is this about Kari? If it is, then I have the right to know."

Linc caught the slight grimace that crossed Reame's face. Linc knew that he wanted to tell him the news in private, so that they could discuss how to tell Tate... Dammit, this news would rock her world.

"Why don't you join Jaeger and Piper, Tate? I'll be back in a minute," Linc suggested, keeping his voice ultracalm.

Her fingernails pushed into his hand like sharp little daggers. "Is it about Kari?" she demanded.

Reame nodded.

"Then I'm coming, too." Tate shot Linc a hard look

when he started to protest. "My sister, Linc, my problem. I am paying Reame's bill, remember?"

Well, no, because he had no intention of letting her do that. But that was an argument for another day. Linc rubbed his jaw and, seeing the fiery determination in Tate's eyes, realized that this was a fight he wasn't going to win.

"I already called for your car," Reame replied. "It's waiting outside, and we'll talk on our way to the airport."

"We're flying?" Linc asked, placing his hand on Tate's lower back as he guided her out of the ballroom.

"Yeah, I called your pilot and told him to file a flight plan," Reame explained, leading the way.

"So where are we going, Reame?" Tate asked, trying to keep the question light, but Linc heard the panic in her voice. "To a jail?" Her voice broke. "A rehab center? A hippy commune?"

Linc helped Tate into her thigh-length black woolen coat. Reame shook his head, his face somber. He looked at Linc, who nodded, silently telling him to get it over with.

Reame placed his hands on Tate's shoulders. and released a heavy sigh. "No, Tate. You're flying to Texas to a hospice about an hour north of Austin. Your sister is there."

"At a hospice? Working there?" Tate asked, puzzled. "No, that can't be right. Kari doesn't do sick people. She wouldn't be working there."

Linc closed his eyes; he'd already made the connection that Tate hadn't. He linked his fingers with hers and squeezed and waited until she looked at him. "Honey, Reame is trying to tell you that she's in the hospice. As a patient."

They were somewhere over Pennsylvania when Tate changed from her ball gown into soft jeans and a thigh-length, moss green jersey that Reame had had Amy pack for her. She scrubbed the makeup from her face and pulled the pins out of her elaborate hairstyle and brushed out the curls, pulling the heavy mess into a tight braid.

Her mind buzzing with both fear and shock, Tate walked back into the main cabin and took a seat opposite Linc, who'd changed into beige chinos and a black sweater over a black-and-white-check shirt. Jo was now back at The Den and watching the kids; Tate trusted her implicitly, and it was a relief not to worry about them. She could focus on Kari and her situation.

As Tate settled into the butter-soft leather chair opposite him, Linc sat up and pushed a glass in her direction. Tate picked up the glass, took a sip and welcomed the burn of rich, expensive cognac. Feeling a little of the icy disbelief melting, she lifted her eyes from the glass to look at Linc.

"Tell me what you know. All of it."

Linc glanced at a folder on the seat next to him but didn't bother to pick it up. He'd read it, absorbed it and his ultrasharp brain wouldn't forget any of it. "Reame's man in Austin tracked down a friend of hers. They've been roommates since Kari split up from Ellie's dad."

"Has she spoken to Kari lately?"

Linc shook his head. "No. Kari refused to allow anyone to visit her, to call for updates on her condition. She didn't want anyone to watch her die."

"We watched her mom die. It was horrible," Tate choked out. "She'd hate people to see her like that."

Tate crossed her legs. "Does she have cancer?"

Linc looked gutted. "Yeah. Stage-four brain cancer. She entered the hospice as soon as she came in from New York after seeing you."

A shudder passed through Tate. "Dear God, that was only a month ago. How did she manage to travel with Ellie, to fly to New York and back?"

"Her friend was with her, apparently. And she was a lot better a month ago. Apparently she has one of the fastest, most aggressive cancers on record, and she went downhill fast."

Tate wrapped her arms around her body and rocked in her chair. Lifting a hand, she gestured for Linc to convey all the information he had. Linc remained silent for a beat before speaking. "From what Reame managed to find out from the friend, she discovered a lump behind her ear when she was pregnant, and she ignored it. When Ellie was six months old, five or so months ago, she had the lump removed and they did a biopsy, and it was found to be malignant. That led to a battery of tests, and they discovered the brain tumor."

"Inoperable?"

"Yeah. They closed her up and told her that she

had, at the maximum, four to six months…if she was lucky."

Tate felt her tears sliding down her face. "God, she must be so scared."

Linc leaned forward, placing his forearms on his thighs, and Tate noticed the grooves beside his mouth, his narrowed eyes and his tense shoulders. Yes, Kari was her sister, but she was also Shaw's mom. He'd loved her once. Linc was hurting, too.

She reached out and covered his bunched fists with her hands, sighing when his fingers linked with hers.

"Her main concern, apparently, was for Ellie's welfare, and she was determined to leave the little girl with you."

"Why didn't she just ask me to look after her like a normal person? Why all this cloak-and-dagger stuff? Why involve you? I don't understand her!" Tate cried.

"Kari never goes directly from A to B, Tate, she always makes a couple of detours. Why be simple when you can complicate the hell out of something?"

Linc made the observation in a voice saturated in frustration but devoid of criticism. Tate's head snapped up, and she watched as he pulled his hands away from hers to rub his face. He swore bitterly, his curses reverberating off the cabin walls.

"I've cursed her six ways to Sunday, Tate, but I swear I never wanted this to happen to her." Linc slammed his head back into the seat and closed his eyes, misery etched on his face. Of course he hadn't, no more than she had.

"Cancer doesn't care who you are, what you do or

what you've done," Tate said, standing up to move across to him. Draping an arm around his neck, she sank down on his lap and curled up against his chest, sighing when his arms went around her. She felt so warm here, so safe. But this was a haven she couldn't linger in, a port she couldn't harbor in for long.

A few months ago she would have imagined giving and receiving comfort from Kari's ex, sitting in his masculine, powerful embrace, thinking that this was her favorite place in the world. She wanted this wonderful, amazing man and his love in her life, but she couldn't ask for it and she certainly didn't deserve it. Love had never treated her kindly. Sure, Linc enjoyed her, he might even like her a little, but she wasn't the stay-at-home-mom, happy-to-be-his-wife woman he said he wanted.

She was never quite what anyone really needed, but at this moment she needed comfort and would settle for a little affection. She wanted to feel alive, to be grateful for what she had. But she did she have a right to take comfort from this man? He was Kari's first, and Tate suspected that a small part of him still loved her. She was the mother of his child; they had a connection she could never have with him. Tate felt the lump in her throat expand and felt the tingle of tears.

This wasn't fair, she raged. None of this was fair, and even less of what was happening made sense. Kari was facing the end of a life lived on her own terms, and, because of that, Tate had become a foster parent after years of being resolutely single. And she'd fallen in love with her sister's ex.

She was questioning everything about her life. Did she really want to return to her busy, lonely, nomadic existence? Did she truly want a life without Linc and Ellie and Shaw? Was she still a rolling stone, or was she turning into a bit of a boulder?

This was all so complicated, Tate thought miserably, pushing herself up from Linc's chest. And she had to start unraveling the mess. To do that she needed to start looking at the situation with clear eyes and a sensible attitude. Right now, she should be concentrating on Kari and her horrible situation. The sensible course of action was to distance herself from Linc, focus on Kari and Ellie and how she was going to navigate the next few weeks.

Tate tried to swing her legs off Linc's lap, but his hand gripped her thigh, keeping her in place. Tate lifted her head to look into his face and saw his need, blazing in his eyes.

"I need you, Tate. I need to feel warm and alive and like the world is not spinning out of control. For some reason, I find that feeling when I'm making love to you."

She heard the plea in his voice, felt the tension in his hand, saw it in his thin lips. She understood his need, she found peace in his arms, too, a solace that took her away from the here and now. And, God, they needed to leave the here and now, just for a little while.

Then Linc slid his hand up her cheek, tunneled his fingers into her hair, and his mouth was on hers, hot and demanding, a little desperate and a lot wild.

His tongue pushed between her lips to mate with hers in long, hot, ravenous strokes that sent shivers and shocks over her skin. God, she needed him. She needed his heat and his virility, to feel the long play of his muscles under her hands, to touch his skin, to have him slide inside her, filling her, completing her.

Linc was the person she'd always want. It would be so easy to hand this situation over to him, to allow him to make the decisions for her, to relinquish control. So easy but that was a slippery slope, and soon she'd lose herself in him. She couldn't do that; she'd worked too hard to find her true authentic self. Being independent allowed her to keep people at arm's length. If she gave that up, she'd allow herself to be vulnerable, to risk her heart. She loved Linc, she did, but she couldn't give him the power to destroy her.

She could only control the now and here, and they had this time, these few hours before they had to deal with a desperately ill Kari. In no time at all she'd have to make some tough decisions, one of which would be to walk away from Linc and Shaw and the life with him she fantasized about. The life she couldn't have.

But for now, for the next four or so hours, she could love him. He was hers.

"Don't walk away from me, Tate. Not now, not yet," Linc said, his voiced gritty from emotion. She jerked her head up, and her eyes met his, filled with raw, palpable desire.

God, how well he knew her.

"I'm in a jet flying at thirty thousand feet," Tate joked but it fell flat. "I'm not going anywhere."

"You know what I mean," Linc growled. "I need all of you, all your hopes and fears. Give them to me, just for the next few hours. Give me you, *all* of you."

She wasn't strong enough to withstand his silent plea for something real, something life affirming, so she gave up the fight. Straddling his lap, she placed tiny butterfly kisses along his jaw, up and over his cheekbone, onto his temple. She rested her forehead against his and looked into his smoky eyes. "Is it wrong to want you, knowing that she is—"

Linc tucked a loose strand of hair behind her ear. "Us enjoying each other isn't going to change what she is going through. Do you want me, honey?"

Tate sighed, her breath sweet on his lips. "I do. So much." She had to work to keep her words of love from passing her lips. He didn't need that from her; he just needed to lose himself in her. And she loved him enough to give him exactly what he needed.

Linc pushed his hips up so that his erection pushed into her. "Then let me make you mine." He closed his eyes as if he were facing a wave of pain. Or pleasure. "I need this, we need this. Here. Now."

"The pilots?" Tate asked, sending an anxious glance at the closed door.

"The do-not-disturb light is on. They'll leave us alone." Linc pulled up her jersey to stroke her sides, his fingers on her ribs just below her breasts. "You feel amazing."

Tate dropped her mouth on his, and their hot, frenzied kiss went on and on, two mouths desperate to mate. Tate pulled his sweater and shirt up his chest, desperate to get her hands on Linc's skin, and they broke their kiss for him to pull the garments over his head. Linc, impatient and demanding, helped her peel her sweater off and then held her away from him to look down at her sheer bra that did nothing to conceal her pointed nipples.

"You are so damn sexy," Linc muttered, bending his head to suck her through the lace. She held the back of his head and arched up into him, lost in his touch, in how incredibly feminine and powerful he made her feel. This was the ultimate aphrodisiac, she thought, having an incredibly sexy man want you with every fiber of his being.

This was what being alive felt like.

Without warning, Linc banded a strong arm around her back and lifted her up, surging to his feet as he did so. Letting her stand, his hands went to the band of her jeans, flipping open the button and pulling down the zipper.

"Take your bra off," he commanded and Tate did as he asked. When her torso was free of the lace, she dragged her breasts across his chest, enjoying the rough hair, the sinewy muscle underneath his skin.

"I want you." She panted, reaching down to palm his erection now throbbing beneath her touch. Linc groaned, pushed her panties and jeans down her hips and steadied her as she kicked off her ballet flats and stepped out of her jeans. Linc pulled her to him, making sure that her most sensitive parts were intimately connected with his fabric-covered erection.

"Get naked," Tate breathed after pulling her mouth off his to speak.

"Shh, baby, slow it down," Linc told her. "We have a couple of hours."

Tate shook her head, and, holding his head in her hands so that he had to look at her, she spoke. *"Now."*

Breaking their contact, Linc pulled off his socks and shoes, stepped out of his pants and groaned when her hand encircled his long, steel-hard length. He felt amazing, all harnessed power. Linc muttered something about a condom and pushed her hand away to slap his against a small cupboard above his head. Ducking his hand inside, he pulled out a strip of foil packets.

Tate grabbed the foil packet from him, tore it open and pulled out the latex sheath. Rolling it onto Linc—accompanied by his grateful groans—she pressed her lips into his chest, holding him with both hands. She didn't like how much she loved making love to him, how much she loved him.

She wished he could love her back, that he could heal her fears, convince her that he'd never hurt her, that he'd never leave her. That there was some way for them to be together.

Linc's hand stilled between her legs. "Tate, honey? You okay?"

Tate flashed him a smile. "I'm grand, why?"

"You tensed and you had a strange look on your face."

Yeah, that's my how-the-hell-am-I-going-to-survive-loving-you face. Tate forced a smile and moved against his hand. She linked her arms around his neck, and when he boosted her up his body, she buried her face in his neck. "Make love to me, Linc."

"That would be my absolute pleasure," he growled, pulling her down to the settee, where he stretched out on top of her, her legs opening to allow him inside. He surged inside her and he filled up every hollow, dark, shadowed part of her. He was her brownstone just off Park Avenue, big and bold and so damn permanent. He was the soil she could imagine planting her roots in, the home she never thought she needed. He was her soft place to fall. He was, Tate thought as he pulled her closer and closer to oblivion, her everything.

Eleven

In the administrator's office in the hospice just north of Austin, Linc managed the introductions and guided Tate to one of the visitors' chairs, watching Kari's doctor as she moved to sit behind her large, paper-strewn desk.

Linc took the chair next to Tate and flicked a glance at her worried face. Her mouth, the amazing mouth he'd kissed with ferocious abandon earlier, was pulled tight, and her body was taut with tension. *Dammit, Kari, sick or not, why couldn't you have just had a conversation like a normal person?*

Why did everything have to be a drama?

Linc listened with half an ear as Dr. Mitchell made small talk with Tate, asking about her childhood with Kari and inquiring about Ellie.

Drama, Kari excelled at it. And that was the difference between the sisters; Tate was a straight shooter, someone who looked at life the way it was and not how she wanted it to be. Was she perfect? No, but he didn't expect her to be. She carried more emotional baggage than she did real luggage. She was wary and insecure but she wasn't flighty, selfish or dramatic, and he...

He loved her.

Linc gripped the arms of his chair and stared down at the carpet below his feet. He'd never expected this, not with Tate, but, yeah, he *loved* her and it felt nothing like he'd expected it to. He'd thought that if he ever fell in love again the feeling would be accompanied by angels singing or African drums. That he'd feel swamped, drowning under the rush of emotion, but he felt none of that. It just felt right.

It felt as if his soul had found its warm spot to curl up in, like he'd found a safe place to shelter from the storm outside. He felt as if he had another source of strength to draw upon, an alternate source of wisdom that was now accessible to him.

This love he felt, this was deep and real and nothing like he'd ever experienced before. It was the phone calls they shared during the day, the silly text messages that got him through those endlessly long, tedious meetings. It was how he felt at the end of the day walking into his house and seeing her there, filling his home with her warmth, her laughter and her perfume. It was the fantastic, mind-blowing sex that always left him aching for more, and it was that indescribable feeling like she was in his corner, utterly and absolutely on his side. He'd started off not trusting her because she was a Harper, but now he trusted her because she was Tate, a fascinating and unique product of her Harper past.

Linc sucked in a deep breath as the realization rolled in that, while he might be in love, she might not be feeling the same. Tate had set objectives for her life, and love and a partnership—in whatever form that took—wasn't something she was looking for. So many people had disappointed her; the people who were supposed to love her best never had, and as a result, she had enormous trust issues. Tate wouldn't easily believe that he was in it for the long haul, that he was prepared to love her and Ellie, for the rest of his life.

He knew that she felt something for him—so he'd just have to take it slow, get her used to the idea that she was exactly where she was meant to be.

And they'd have to find a way to work around her need to be independent, her career. He wanted her to have it all; he didn't want her to sacrifice a damn thing for him. It was the twenty-first century; if he could be both a dad and businessman, then Tate could have her career and be a mother and a wife.

Linc rolled his head on his shoulders, trying to ease some of the tension in the cords of his neck. Dr. Mitchell looked at each of them, and then leaned back in her chair, her expression gentle and sad.

"Ms. Harper, I regret to tell you that your sister passed away early this morning. I am so very sorry."

Linc closed his eyes as sorrow seeped into him. Yeah, Kari drove him nuts but she had given him an amazing son. *Kari, rest easy.*

Linc clenched his hands around the arm of his chair before placing his arm around Tate's very stiff shoulders. He looked at her and tried to gauge her reaction. To Linc it looked like she'd shrunk in on herself; she looked smaller and frailer. But it was her expression that scared him or, more accurately, it was her lack of expression.

For the first time, he couldn't discern any emotion in her eyes. There was no sadness, no anger, no regret. Linc turned in his chair and forced his fingers through hers, and he grew concerned when she didn't respond. She'd retreated to a place where he couldn't reach her, Linc suddenly realized. This was the same place she'd said she retreated to during her childhood, when the pressure and pain of living with her mother and sister became too much. The same place she went to when her father disappointed her time and time again.

Tate was on her island and he couldn't get to her…

"I have tried to contact you, but your phone has been going straight to messages for the last six hours."

"I was at a function and didn't think to turn it back on," Tate told her tonelessly.

Dr. Mitchell cleared her throat, and Linc looked at her, his eyebrows raised. "Kari deteriorated quickly when she got here. It was almost as if she stopped fighting."

"I have to organize her funeral," Tate said, staring straight ahead.

"Kari left explicit instructions. She didn't want a funeral and her body is already on its way to a home to be cremated."

She made arrangements for her funeral but not for her kids? Linc shook his head. "Her ashes?" Tate asked in a monotone voice.

"She ordered the funeral home to dispose of them," Dr. Mitchell replied, staring down at the folder she'd opened on her desk. "She did, however, leave a will."

"A will? Kari?" Linc asked, unable to keep the skepticism from his voice.

Dr. Mitchell nodded. "It's part of the admission process. We insist that our patients sort out their affairs."

Linc frowned as a thought suddenly occurred to him. "How did she pay you? The Kari we know—*knew*—didn't have the cash to pay for a private facility."

"We do take pro bono cases. Kari was one of those."

Hearing that, Linc immediately decided that he'd leave a check to cover Kari's expenses. She was, after all, the mother of his child.

Dr. Mitchell looked at Tate. "Kari wanted me to explain her wishes, but if you'd prefer to deal with a lawyer, then you can."

Tate's eyes had yet to leave the doctor's face. "No, you can tell me," she said, her voice even but still devoid of emotion.

"Before she died, Kari did make arrangements to have Ellie adopted. In fact, she worked with an adoption agency and preapproved a couple for Ellie to go to."

Ellie wasn't going anywhere! She was Tate's. And his. He couldn't lose his two girls.

"Kari wanted to give you the option of adopting Ellie, as well. Essentially, the paperwork at the adoption agency has been completed. It just needs either your signature or the Goldbergs' signatures, and Ellie has a new family."

"Did..." Tate cleared her throat. "Did Kari indicate where she'd prefer Ellie to go?"

Dr. Mitchell shook her head. "She said either of the options was fine. Essentially, she left the choice up to you."

"I see..." Tate softly replied and Linc released a sharp breath, desperate to know what was going through Tate's mind right now.

Oh, Tate, come back. Feel angry, feel sad. Please, don't shut down, and, God, don't shut me out.

"Everything you need to proceed is in the folder, Tate." Dr. Mitchell closed the folder and handed it to Tate, who took it with a rock-steady hand. "I am very sorry for your loss."

Linc placed his hand under Tate's elbow and felt her jerk her arm away. He frowned at her profile, set in stone, and felt her sliding away.

He silently cursed, hot, heavy words that gave him no relief. He would fight as hard as he could, for her, for them, for the family they were in the process of building, but if she chose to run, there would be little he could do about it. Running away was, after all,

what she always did when life became complicated or
people demanded more than what she wanted to give.

It would be interesting to see how he coped with
the tsunami of pain that was bound to follow her de-
parture.

Hi Tate!
Just to let you know that we'd love to have you host
our new, US-based travel show. It's a show devel-
oped for your unique delivery style and personality
and we're excited to work closely with you on this
project. Details and the contract to follow and let me
know when we can meet.

Tate read the email again and tossed her phone
onto the bed and shoved two hands into her messy
hair. She'd been back in The Den for two days, and
she felt as if she was operating on fresh air and emotion. Her sister, the person she'd both loved and hated,
was dead.

Her daughter was now Tate's responsibility.

She was in love with Kari's ex.

Kari was dead…

And she had the offer of a new job…

Tate rested her forehead against the cool wall of
her bedroom, too numb to think, still too stunned to
cry. A part of her wanted to scream, to hurl curses at
God and Fate, but mostly she just wanted to curl up
into a ball and go to sleep.

Is this what an emotional meltdown felt like, Tate
wondered, panic creeping up her throat. For the first

time ever, she didn't know what to do, how to act. Should she run? Should she stay? Should she talk to Linc or just pick up her niece and her stuff and leave?

Talk or run? Stay or go?

Her indecision terrified her.

"Hey, sweetheart."

Tate turned around and looked at Linc, leaning his big shoulder into the frame of the door. So solid, so protective, a guardian through and through. God, it would be so easy to throw herself on Linc's broad chest, feel his arms banding around her, silently assuring her that she was safe, that he'd protect her. Because that's what Linc did, the core of who he was. At eleven he'd scooped up the Ballantyne siblings and placed them under his wing, determined to shelter them through their grief. He was Connor's heir apparent, and he felt utterly responsible for the well-being of Ballantyne International. He was insanely protective of Shaw and still worried about his grown-up, very capable siblings.

Linc saw himself as a white knight, and she and Ellie roused his every protective instinct. What she saw in Linc's eyes was not love or affection; it was his need to watch over and care for those around him.

Tate placed her palm on the wall. As much as she wanted Linc, physically, she couldn't allow herself to lean on him. She needed to stand on her own two feet. Find some perspective, some clarity. Distancing herself would give her that.

It would allow her to make smart decisions, decisions that would stand the test of time. Kari and her mom were the queens of hasty, off-the-cuff choices, and most of them had blown up in their faces. She wouldn't do that; Ellie was too important, too precious to treat lightly.

Tate felt Linc's hand on the back of her neck and closed her eyes when he kissed her temple.

"How you doing, sweetheart?" he asked, and Tate's heart sighed. She fought the urge to turn her face into his neck, to wrap her arms around his waist and to rest there for a while. She was exhausted; emotionally and physically drained.

Tate forced her feet backwards, and Linc's hand dropped from her neck. "I'm..." Sad? Gutted? Emotionally whipped? "I'm okay."

Linc frowned at her. "Really? Because I'm feeling like someone used me as a floor rag."

He lifted a hand to her face and ran his thumb under her eyes, across her cheekbone. God, she felt as if being touched by him was what she was put on this earth to do. Tate jerked her head at the thought and stepped back again, shaking her head. *You're not doing this, Tate, you're not going down that road. Distance, dammit!* Creating distance was her best coping mechanism, the way she avoided disappointment and heartbreak. And bad decisions.

Distance had served her well in the past.

"I've had a job offer," Tate blurted, keeping her voice flat.

Linc's eyebrows rose and a muscle jumped in his cheek. His hand fell to his side. "Really? Where?"

"I don't know too much about it except that it's a US-based travel program, which will be a change."

"What about Ellie? How are you going to manage her and the job?"

Linc threw up his hands in frustration when she didn't respond. He correctly interpreted her silence. "Oh, come on, Tate! You can't seriously be thinking about giving her up. She belongs with you, any fool can see that—"

"How do I support her? She doesn't come with a trust fund, Linc! I have to clothe and feed her and educate her! How do I do that? If I give up my career for her, where do I find another job where I can be with her and support her?"

"Here, at The Den," Linc stated. It took a moment for the words to register, for the pennies to drop.

Tate frowned, not sure that she'd heard him correctly. "You're offering me the nanny job?"

"I trust you with Shaw. I like having you in my house, and I'd pay you well."

She loved Shaw and Ellie, but there were so many places she still wanted to see, to share with the world. She adored her job, and he was asking her to walk away from it? "Are you completely nuts?"

"Probably. But I'm also in love with you, and I'm trying to finding a way to make you stay," Linc said, in an annoyingly calm voice. "I thought I'd ease you into living with me…us."

Tate placed her fist into her sternum, utterly shell-shocked by his prosaic announcement. Linc just held her eyes, his hands in his pockets, waiting for her reaction.

Tate lifted her fist to her mouth, her eyes blurring with tears. She heard his words, but she couldn't trust them, she couldn't allow herself to take the risk of believing him.

He couldn't, shouldn't love her... She wasn't what he needed. He needed a woman who was completely and utterly focused on him and on their life at The Den; she'd always have one eye on the horizon, dreaming about another place she wanted to explore. Linc deserved a woman who gave him exactly what he needed and wanted, and while she loved him, she was terrified that he'd one day realize that he'd mistaken his need to protect her and Ellie with love.

Besides, she needed to leave, to test her theory that distance gave her perspective. Would what she felt for Linc be as strong away from him as it was with him? Somehow she thought not.

"We agreed to keep it simple, Linc. To not let it get emotional. You told me I'm not what you wanted! You want a domestic goddess, a stay-at-home mom, a compliant wife."

"I'm pretty sure I never mentioned the word *compliant*," Linc muttered. He rubbed the back of his neck, obviously frustrated.

"You told me that I deserve to be happy, and you, for some reason, make me happy." Linc pulled his hands from his pockets and reached for her, but Tate danced out of his grip, knowing that if he touched her, she'd never leave his arms again.

She had to—she had to run, she had to put the distance she needed between them.

"Make some ties, Tate, commit to me, to us. Stop protecting yourself from life and love," Linc said, his eyes sad but determined. "Be brave, Tate. Love me, embrace the life I'm offering you."

Tate wished she could, but it wasn't possible. Tate slowly shook her head. She couldn't risk hurting him, hurting herself. No, it was better if she left now, while both their hearts were still, sort of, intact.

When she had distance from him, when she wasn't confused by all the emotions swirling between them, she'd feel differently, she'd feel as she always had: that she was right in her belief that she was better off alone, that she didn't need love in her life.

Tate knew how to run away; she knew what she had to do.

She'd pack up and find a hotel, which is what she should have done weeks ago when she first acquired Ellie. She'd meet with the adoption agency and the Goldbergs and see if Kari was right, if being with them would be the right choice for Ellie. If they could give her a good life, no, a *wonderful* life, she'd hand over custody, hoping that the Goldbergs would allow her to have contact with Ellie going forward.

She would take the new job she'd been offered, and life would return to a new type of normal.

Tate closed her eyes against the wave of pain at the thought of not having Ellie or Linc or Shaw in her life, but she knew it would pass, that each day would get better. Keeping it simple, being on her own, was the way she had to live.

It had worked for ten years; it would work again.

She had to do this. She had to tell him.

Linc beat her to it. He lifted a hand, his eyes steel gray. "Don't bother saying anything, I can see the answer in your eyes. You're going to run, because that's what you Harper girls do."

"It's for the best, Linc."

"BS! Instead of staying, talking it out, working it out, you're running." Linc linked his hands behind his head, the cords in his neck tight with frustration. "You kept telling me you were different from Kari, Tate."

"I am."

Linc shook his head and flashed her a cold smile. "Are you? You took what I offered, and when it became a little uncomfortable, a little heated, you decide to walk, run, whatever the hell you Harpers call this."

He's trying to hurt you, wanting and needing to lash out, Tate told herself, but his words still whipped her with the ferocity of an Arctic storm.

"It's not like that, Linc." she said, silently begging him to believe her.

"Funny, it feels exactly the same." Linc strode over to the door. He placed his hand on the door frame and gripped it tight. "Can you be gone by the time Shaw comes home from pre-K? I don't want him upset any more than he needs to be."

She didn't want it to end like this. "Linc—"

Linc spun around, and his lightning-filled eyes

pinned her to the spot. "All I've ever wanted, Tate, was someone to stay. No matter how hard it got, just to stand next to me. And, because I'm such a flippin' fool, I thought that person might be you."

Tate, her heart cracking, watched him walk through the doorway, heard the clatter of Linc's feet on the stairs and then, a minute later, the heavy, hard thud of the front door slamming closed.

Tate sobbed as she watched his hunched figure walk down the sidewalk away from the house, walking out of her life.

Just as she'd told him to.

Twelve

Two weeks later, Ellie, sitting on the carpet in the Goldbergs' comfortable lounge, held a small feather duster and waved it in front of an orange cat's nose. The cat swiped the duster with its white paw, causing Ellie to release a girly laugh.

This is what Ellie needed, Tate thought. Two parents, comfortably well-off, a nice home, a cat. Two people who absolutely adored her, who would sell their souls to raise this precious, precious human being. Giving them Ellie would be the right thing to do, the kind thing to do; it made sense in every corner of the universe.

Ellie chuckled again and lifted her eyes to meet Tate's, the perfect little person demanding she share the fun. Tate felt her heart roller-coaster around her chest, trying to resist the urge to scoop Ellie into her arms and chant "mine, mine, mine."

Sandra and George both had college degrees and good jobs; they had extensive family and lots of nephews and nieces so Ellie would have lots of cousins to play with. They had a solid support group, and, best of all, they were completely open to Tate visiting Ellie, to allowing her to be part of her life going forward.

They were an excellent choice; she could see why Kari was so taken with them. Ellie's laugh washed over her, and Tate closed her eyes. Just put them out of their misery, give them the gift of Ellie and get on with your life, the life she'd spent the last two weeks planning. She was taking the job she'd been offered, had accepted the very hefty salary, and had demanded, and been given, a lot more creative control. This was her show, and she was going to put her stamp on it.

The show had to be stunningly successful; she was sacrificing everything she loved for it and her career. It had better be worth it.

Tate folded her hands over her stomach and stared at Ellie. She had just two weeks before she had to fly out to Aspen to shoot the first episode, and after that she'd pass custody of Ellie to the Goldbergs. She just had to get them to sign the adoption papers and arrange for them to have temporary custody until the adoption was court approved.

She was doing what was best for Ellie, but how could she walk away knowing that Ellie wouldn't be a daily part of her life? How could she miss the first time she walked, her first proper word, the toddler tantrums and her first day at school? She wanted to wipe away tears caused by snotty friends, childhood scrapes or stupid boys. She wanted to help choose her prom dress, go shopping with her, watch her marry, have kids of her own.

She wanted it all. She wanted Ellie. She wanted Shaw, as well. And Linc. She needed her family, as cobbled together as it was. She needed to be the mom, the wife, the lover… God, if she couldn't be any of those, then she'd settle for being the damn nanny.

She just wanted to be with them, around them. And even if Linc wasn't interested in her anymore— she'd noticed that that he hadn't called her once—she could still be Ellie's mom. Yes, it meant sacrificing her career as a travel presenter, but surely there was something else she could do to earn money? Maybe she could arrange culinary tours for travel agencies or become a travel agent or write for a foodie magazine. She could work at night, when Ellie slept; anything was possible if she tried.

But if she allowed this little girl to slip away because she was too damn scared to be her mommy, she'd regret it for the rest of her life. If she walked away from Linc, from Shaw because she was scared, because she put her career and her independence before the people who made her heart sing, she'd never forgive herself. She loved Linc, she loved the family they'd started to become.

She'd been so convinced that she'd needed distance, that she was better off alone, that she didn't need love in her life. She was so full of it…

If anything, she'd quickly realized that she'd been completely, comprehensively, *asininely* wrong. It turned out that she needed love and intimacy, she needed Linc to be the best version of herself. She was a shadow of the person she was with Linc, loving Linc. He made her stronger, wiser, simply better.

She'd messed up badly, and she'd hurt Linc, hurt what they had by running away, instead of planting her feet on the ground. She'd hit him hard by doing exactly what Kari did, leaving him because she didn't have the guts to stay.

She'd fulfilled his worst fears about her, and she couldn't be more ashamed of herself. She kept telling him that she was nothing like her sister, but when the chips were down, she was. For that, at the very least, she had to apologize. At the very best, and if Fate was a little kind, maybe they could talk, maybe she could find a way back into his arms. She'd swallow her pride, grovel and beg if she needed to. She just wanted to have contact with him, somehow, in some way.

Ellie waved the feather duster, her bright smile showing off one bottom tooth. "Ma…ma."

Tate placed her hand on her heart and nodded. Yes, she was her mama. Maybe not by blood but by love…

Tate bit her lip and turned to look at Sandra and George who were looking sad but not surprised. "I'm sorry, I can't. She's mine."

Sandra leaned forward and patted her knee. "We

know. We've known it from the first moment you walked in the door."

Tate released a half sob, half laugh. "Then why did you let me come back?"

George shrugged. "We hoped that we were wrong."

"I'm so sorry," Tate said, standing up. "I didn't mean to lead you on, to play games with your expectations. I really didn't know for sure until a minute ago."

George nodded and stood up. Sandra bent down to pick up Ellie, gave her a quick cuddle and her eyes misted over with tears when Ellie leaned toward Tate, her body language telling them all where she wanted to be. Tate settled her on her hip and bent her knees to snag her bag from the settee.

"I hope you find a baby soon," Tate said, feeling embarrassed and more than a little guilty.

Sandra nodded. "Goodbye, Tate. Goodbye, Ellie."

At the door George shook her hand and didn't bother to walk her down the path to the road. Sucking in cold air, Tate pulled up the hood on Ellie's little snowsuit and kissed her cheek. "I love you, my darling El."

Ellie patted her cheek and buried her face in Tate's neck.

"So, what the hell do we do now, El? I'm open for suggestions." Tate tipped her head, pretending that Ellie had answered her. "Do you think that we should find Linc, that we should go to him and tell him that I was wrong, that we miss him and that we love him?"

Elli laughed and blew Tate a kiss. She'd take that as a yes. "Right, any ideas on how to do that?"

Ellie rested her head on Tate's collarbone and within minutes she was a dead weight in her arms, fast asleep on her chest. That, Tate decided, was her daughter's way of telling her that she'd created the mess they were in and that she'd have to fix it.

Well, she'd try.

Linc ran down the steps to the kitchen for the third time that night and wearily took the glass of whiskey Reame held out to him. Shaw was acting up tonight, just as he had been for every night since Tate left two weeks ago. It felt like forty damned years.

God, he was furious that she'd left him to deal with a confused little boy who thought he'd done something wrong to chase her away. He was incensed that she'd confirmed his worst fears about her, that, like Kari, she bailed when life got sticky.

He'd genuinely believed she was better than that. Then again, he hadn't exactly excelled at getting his point across that night. He'd hadn't taken the time to explain that he wanted her any way he could get her, that he didn't expect her to sacrifice a damn thing for him, that she could have her career, that she didn't need to change anything to become the woman he thought he might, one day, want. She was all he wanted, exactly as she was.

But she'd run and he found that hard to forget. Or forgive. She'd hit him exactly where it hurt the most.

"If you grip that glass any harder it's going to shatter," Reame told him in a mild voice.

Linc looked around his living room and saw that, in between him running upstairs to soothe an upset Shaw, his siblings had arrived. Yeah, not what he needed.

Tate was missing from his house and his life, and, despite his anger and disappointment, he still needed her. He needed her in his arms, kissing his son and her daughter good-night, making love to him when the kids were asleep. He missed Ellie, missed his happy little girl. Because she was his, as much as Shaw was. But most of all, he missed Tate with every fiber of his being.

He never felt the same sort of constant ache when Kari left; he'd been pissed and annoyed and sad on Shaw's behalf, but he hadn't felt like someone was using his heart as a hockey puck. Linc stared at his drink before lifting it to his mouth, grimacing at the awful taste of his favorite ten-year-old rare whiskey.

God, he felt like a shadow of himself.

Reame placed a hard hand on his back and guided him toward the sitting area. His pal pushed him down into the vacant seat next to Sage. Linc wanted to tell him to back the hell off, but he didn't have the energy. Since she left he'd had the minimum amount of sleep. At least he could blame his red-rimmed eyes on lack of sleep and not on the tears he refused to let anyone see.

His fault for falling in love with another Harper woman.

Reame sat on the arm of Beck's chair. "So, what are you going to do about her?" he demanded, finally acknowledging the mammoth in the room.

Linc stared out of the window to the garden and noticed that it was snowing... God, he hoped they were warm. Of course they were, he mocked himself. This was the woman who looked after herself all over the world; she knew how to take care of herself. *She doesn't need you...*

"Nothing," Linc replied in an I'm-not-discussing-her tone of voice.

"Wimp" Beck mocked.

Linc glared at him, but Beck just grinned, amused. There had been a time when a watch-it look from him meant something, but no longer.

"There are so many unanswered questions," Sage mused, tucking her feet up under her, leaning her shoulder into Linc's.

"She left. That's the end of the story. No additional questions or explanations needed," Linc bit out.

"You can growl all you want, but we all know that you are desperate to know whether she gave Ellie up for adoption and whether she's signed a new contract."

"She's keeping Ellie."

Linc sat up and looked at Reame, narrowing his eyes at his oldest friend.

"She can't keep Ellie and do the show, so that means she'll be sacrificing her job. She loves her job," Linc stated. *Dammit, Tate! If you'd stayed, you could've had it all.*

"All I know is that she's keeping Ellie," Reame reiterated.

"And how do you know that?" Linc demanded.

Reame returned his hot look with one of his own. "Why do you want to know? You are the one who let her go."

"She left," Linc said, his teeth grinding together. "I told her I loved her, but she still left. Reame, dammit, tell me!"

Reame, the bastard, tossed him a smug smile. "I called her earlier today and asked her."

Jaeger laughed and Reame shrugged. "PI skills 101," he explained.

"So, bro," Beck asked, his ankle on his knee, "are you going to man up and go to her and try and sort out this mess?"

Linc kept his eyes on Reame, and Reame responded with a it's-time-to-get-your-ass-into-gear look. "She's not Kari, Linc," Reame stated.

Linc nodded. "I know."

She wasn't. Linc felt his head swim. The last of his resentment toward Kari faded away, and images of his time with Tate flashed on the big screen inside his head... Tate making cupcakes with Shaw, cuddling Ellie, her bright smile when she saw him for the first time at the end of the day. Tate naked, her expression blissful as he ran his hands over her fine skin, down her hip, between her thighs.

Tate, messy haired and bighearted. Tate in tears, crying over Kari. Tate...

Just Tate. His world didn't make sense without her in it. He needed her in his world.

Linc looked down when he felt Sage patting him down with a dishcloth, Beck standing over him and picking glass off his chest. Reame was holding his hand, and suddenly he realized that blood was dripping from his palm onto the leg of his jeans, some drops finding their way onto the laminated wooden floor under his feet. Linc looked at his hand again and noticed that he had a two-inch shard of glass sticking out of his hand and that he wasn't feeling a damn thing.

"I'm going to pull this out, and then I'll decide if we need to take you to the emergency room, bro," Reame told him.

"Does it hurt, Linc? Are you okay?"

Linc looked at Sage and managed a smile. "Not as much as my heart does."

"Can you fix it?" Sage asked him, picking up the bottom piece of his broken glass from the floor by his feet.

"My heart or my hand?" Linc nodded decisively. "Damn right I can fix both."

"Excellent news," Reame said, examining his hand. "The not-so-excellent news is that this is deep, and you need stitches."

"Crap." Linc looked at the kitchen towel that Beck was pressing into his hand. "I was going to leave you lot to babysit, and I was going to find Tate."

"Not tonight you're not," Reame told him. He gripped Linc's uninjured hand and hauled him to his feet. "You have a couple of painkillers and at least six stitches in your immediate future."

Linc looked from his very bloody hand to his oldest friend. Screw the blood and stitches. "Take me to her, Reame. I know that you know where she is."

Reame looked at his siblings, his eyebrows raised. "We need a translator. Do we know anyone who speaks fluid idiot?"

"Very funny," Linc retorted. He saw the commanding officer look on Reame's face and grimaced. "Is there any point in arguing?"

"You can, but it's not going to change the outcome," Reame, the bastard, cheerfully told him. "One, or all your sibs, will stay here to look after Shaw."

Linc watched as more blood fell from his hand to the floor. "Damn, now it hurts."

"Since you crushed a crystal glass in your hand, it damn well should," Jaeger told him. "Moron."

His hand was on fire, his heart was battered, and he had to put up with crap from his siblings? On what planet was that fair? Linc sent Jaeger a screw-you look. "Remind me to kick your ass."

"You and whose army, sweetheart?"

Linc snatched up his cell and headed for the stairs. "Idiots," he muttered, taking the fresh kitchen towel from Reame and pushing it into his gushing, burning hand. "Idiots everywhere."

Jaeger's chuckle drifted to him. "And you are their king."

* * *

After running scenarios and practicing what she wanted to say, it still took Tate most of the evening to gather her courage to go to Linc. Finally, a little after eleven at night, Tate, using the key she had never bothered to return, let herself into The Den. Navigating the house by feel, she carried a sleeping Ellie up to the third floor and placed her in the crib she'd been sleeping in up until a couple of weeks before.

Slipping out of her coat, Tate grabbed the baby monitor off the bedside table and crept down the stairs to the second floor. She opened Shaw's door and walked over to his bed, dropping down to kiss his cheek. Taking a deep breath and wondering, not for the first time, whether she was completely nuts coming over to talk to Linc so late, she eased open the door to Linc's bedroom and frowned at his empty bed. So… Huh, avoiding explanations by slipping into bed with him wasn't an option.

So much for that fantasy.

After running back up to the third floor, Tate found Sage fast asleep in her bedroom.

If Sage was looking after Shaw, then Linc was out.

Out working? Or out drinking? Clubbing? God, *dating*?

Tate walked down the stairs and sat down on the settee next to the front door. What if Linc came home with a woman, what would she do? How would she cope? What if he'd changed his mind about her staying? What if he didn't want to talk?

She felt her insides ripping apart, and she was about to run up the stairs and collect Ellie when she heard low male voices and a key in the front door. Tate watched the door swing open, and then Reame and Linc walked in, shrugging out of their coats.

Linc's eyes widened when he saw her, and his eyes flashed with an emotion she didn't immediately recognize. Relief? Surprise? A combination of both?

Tate immediately noticed his bandaged hand and his bloody shirt and bounded forward. She touched his chest and looked into his pain-filled eyes. "God, are you okay?"

Linc's eyes just bounced from feature to feature as if he couldn't quite believe she was there. "You're here. Hi."

Tate touched his cheek and smiled. "Hi back." Worried, she looked at Reame. "Is he okay?"

Reame nodded. "Crushed a glass in his hand and he needed a whole bunch of stitches." Reame held out a pill bottle which he dropped into Tate's hand. "He did a good job of slicing his hand so he needs to take two of these in the morning. That's if you are going to be here in the morning."

Tate held his eyes as her fingers slipped into Linc's uninjured hand. "I plan on being here."

Reame cocked his head at her, his gaze probing. "You staying this time, Tate?"

Tate nodded. "If Linc wants me to."

Linc didn't speak. He just opened the front door

and jerked his head, a clear gesture for Reame to leave. Reame took his time picking up his coat and pulling it on, his eyes filled with amusement.

"Coffee would be nice. It's cold out there," Reame teased and Tate frowned. She liked Reame, she did, but she needed to be alone with Linc.

Linc scowled at Reame and gestured for him to leave. "Out!"

"Such gratitude," Reame grumbled good-naturedly as he moved out into the night. Tate called a soft goodbye but wasn't sure if Reame heard her because Linc quickly slammed the door behind him.

Linc turned back to her and placed his hands on her biceps, and suddenly Tate was inhaling his cologne, looking into his smoldering eyes. She was home...

"Did you mean that?" he demanded. "About staying?"

Tate lifted her hands to rest them on his chest.

"Yes, I'll stay." Tate pulled her bottom lip between her teeth. "If you want me."

"I'll always want you, Tate."

She released her lip, and Linc swiped his thumb across the skin to ease the sting. He pulled her closer and slid his hand around the back of her neck, using his thumb to lift her face up. "We need to talk, but we'll get to that. But first, this."

His mouth covered hers, and Tate felt his cool lips on hers. His sigh hit her mouth, and she instinctively opened hers, and his tongue slipped inside, a hot, slow slide. She'd missed him, missed his clever mouth and his ever-changing eyes, his big body, both clothed and naked.

She'd felt adrift these past couple of weeks, more alone than she'd ever felt in her life. Her world had faded to grayscale, to wishy shades of gray. Life with Linc, with the kids, his and hers, infused her life with color. She felt alive with him; just sitting next to him made her feel like the best version of herself.

God, she loved him. She could stand here, on her tiptoes, and be kissed by him for the rest of her life. If that was all she could have of him, she'd take it.

Linc pulled away from her and rested his forehead on hers, his hand cradling her cheek. "That was about fifteen days, eight hours and ten minutes overdue."

"I have no idea what's happening here, but as long as you keep kissing me, I'm good."

Linc grinned, and his smile had her heart doing backflips. "FYI, I plan on kissing you for a long, long time. In fact, that talk is going to be delayed for a while, because I plan to kiss you for the rest of the night."

Tate allowed Linc to lead her to the stairs, her hand firmly clasped by his uninjured one. "Just kiss me?" She mock pouted. "Nothing else?"

Linc stopped and turned around to look down at her, and Tate's heart hitched at the pure emotion she saw on his face. "Tate, I'd give you the world if I could, right now. Seeing you standing in my hallway is all my Christmases and birthdays rolled into one. The only time I've ever come so close to feeling as happy was when Connor showed me the adoption papers stating that I was officially a Ballantyne. There's nothing I wouldn't give you." Linc squeezed her hand. "Come upstairs with me."

Didn't he realize that she'd go anywhere, do anything for him, with him? Tate slowly nodded and ran up the stairs with him.

Thirteen

The smell of good coffee pulled Tate from a heavy sleep, and she woke up slowly, immediately looking for the source. As her eyes focused, Linc sat down on the side of the bed, Ellie on his knee, her beautiful face full of smiles. Having been the focus of Linc's exquisite attention for most of the night, Tate was full of smiles, as well.

Tate pushed herself up and leaned over to nuzzle Ellie's cheek. "Mornin', baby."

Linc raised an amused eyebrow when she leaned back. "And where's my 'morning, baby'?"

Tate overexaggerated her sigh and hooked her hand around his neck to pull him down for an open-mouth kiss. "Mornin' baby," she said, her voice husky with laughter.

Linc grinned. "Much better."

"Where's Shaw?" Tate asked, placing her hand over her mouth to hide her yawn.

"Still asleep." Linc pushed the cup of coffee into her hand. "Drink this, have a shower and I'll wake Sage up and tell her that she's on kid duty for a little while. Last night was amazing, but we really need to talk."

Oh, God, he looked and sounded so solemn. Had he changed his mind? She couldn't bear it if the happiness, the hope she'd been feeling, was suddenly snatched out of her hands. Fear and insecurity, hot and hard, bubbled up her throat. "Yes, okay."

Tate pushed her hair back as Linc stood up. Tate took a moment to admire her sexy man dressed in a berry-colored sweater and dark pants. She couldn't wait… She couldn't stand the tension for one more minute, so she pushed a nervous hand into her hair and sent him a troubled look.

Tate spoke, and the butterflies in her stomach took flight. "Did you mean what you said, on the stairs?"

"Are you doubting me? This?"

Tate gave him a quick nod. She looked at the door and fought her instinct to run. "A little. I'm feeling hopeful and happy, and I'm scared it's all going to evaporate." Tate looked into her coffee cup and told herself that running was no longer an option. Yes, she was risking her heart and her future, but Linc was worth it. She had to talk, to lay it on the line; she had to trust him with all that she was. Her hopes and her fears. "I'm scared that you are confused about what you want, I'm worried that you might change your mind about me—" Tate gestured to Ellie "—about us."

It wasn't one person walking into his life and hoping to stay; it was two.

Linc sat down again, rested his chin on Ellie's head and sent her a steady look. "I've been up for hours, Tate. So far, I've contacted my lawyer to get the paperwork started on all the adoptions that need to happen to make us a proper family—me to adopt Ellie, you to adopt Ellie and Shaw. I've contacted an agency to find an experienced nanny. I've also spoken to Jo, told her that you're back, have asked her to look after the kids for a couple of hours here and there so that you and I can have some alone time. I think we deserve that. I had to run to my office to get something out of my safe—does all that sound like I'm confused about you and what I want?"

Tate, unable to take in all the implications of his speech, just stared at him. Linc leaned down, Ellie in his arms, and brushed his lips against hers. "What about what you want, Tate?"

She swallowed, desperately looking for some moisture in her mouth. "I want it all, Linc. I want you and the kids and..."

"And what, honey?"

Tate tapped her finger against her coffee cup and forced herself to be honest. "I want my career. I love what I do, but if the choice was between you and the kids and my career, then I choose you. I can live without my career. I can't live without you and the kids." She wrinkled her nose. "But a part of me still wants to take this work opportunity even though I under-stand that might not be possible or feasible or realis-tic." She bit her bottom lip. "Or not what you want."

"Because you think that I want a stay-at-home mother for my wife, a wife who knows her place?"

Tate, not sure how to respond, just shrugged and stared down into her cup of rapidly cooling cof-fee. She felt Linc's finger pushing her chin up, and she gasped at the emotion blazing from his eyes. "I thought that was what I wanted, Tate, but I was so damn wrong. All I need is for you to be happy. If tak-ing the job makes you happy, then do it. Take it. In fact, I insist that you do."

God, he made it sound so simple, but it wasn't. "Linc, if I took the job, I'd be away from home a few days every week for a good six months. That's a lot of time away."

Linc looked stubborn. "Our relationship is not about sacrifices, sweetheart. It's about compromises and being organized. And I have enough money at my disposal that I can organize the hell out of any situation."

"Tell me what you are thinking," Tate begged, ut-terly amused by the idea that she could have her man and her kids and her career.

"I meant to tell you that I never intended for you to give up your career. If I can have mine, you can have yours. That's why I mentioned that I contacted an agency to find us a nanny. We'll find someone we all like, and some weeks the nanny and the kids will travel with you, some weeks I will. Maybe with the nanny, depending on my work load, maybe without. Some weeks, depending on your work load, the kids will stay here with me. It's all figure-outable."

It was, Tate thought, her heart expanding with excitement and delight. Together they could do it all. Tate curled her hand around the back of Linc's neck and pulled his head down so that she could brush her lips against his.

Before they went any further, she had to apologize, to ask for his forgiveness for making such a massive mistake by running when she should have planted her feet next to him and stayed. "Linc, I'm sorry I left. So sorry."

Linc tipped his head. "Do you plan on doing it again?" he asked, his voice heart-attack serious.

"No." Tate placed her hand on her heart and shook her head. He had to believe her, she couldn't bear it if he didn't. "God, no! I promise."

Linc's eyes filled with relief, and the corners of his mouth quirked upward. "Then we're good."

"Thank you." Tate breathed the words against his mouth, desperately wanting to thank him for making all her dreams come true. "Thank you for being wonderful and thoughtful and sensitive to my needs. Thank you for giving me my career. Thank you for forgiving me for running away." Tate's eyes filled with tears.

"Thank you for loving Ellie. For loving me," she said, her voice choked with emotion.

Linc wiped away a tear with his thumb before dropping his forehead to rest it on hers. "I'm going to spend the rest of my life loving you, Tate. Because you, more than anyone else I know, are so worthy of being loved."

Linc pulled back and tapped her nose. "Take a shower and I'll see you downstairs. We'll start planning the rest of our lives over breakfast."

"Sounds good," Tate murmured. "Actually, no, that's the sound of all my dreams coming true."

She hadn't told Linc that she loved him yet.

The thought hit Tate as she walked down the stairs twenty minutes later. How could she have neglected such an important detail? She did love him, with every fiber of her being. She hoped he knew that, but in case he didn't, she'd tell him as soon as she saw him.

He'd given her so much, yet she still hadn't given him the words he needed the most. God, she sucked at being in love, but she would learn. She was as determined to make Linc as happy as he made her.

On an impulse Tate sat down on the bottom stair and looked around the hallway, her hand running over the polished step next to her thigh. She loved this house, she realized, and it wasn't because it was situated on one of the best streets in Manhattan or because it was worth a fortune. She loved it because all the people she loved lived here. Tate looked up at the portrait of Connor on the wall opposite her, taking in his patrician face and his merry blue Ballantyne eyes. She was sorry she'd never met Linc's father, but she thought she would've liked him. So many generations of Ballantynes had grown up in this house, and it sounded like Linc had plans for Shaw and Ellie to do the same.

Love, she felt, had seeped into the bones of this house, into the walls, into the foundations. Sometimes she felt that she could hear whispered laughter, hot spots of warmth, the suggestion of spiritual energy. She didn't think the place was haunted, but she did feel like the previous occupants had left a little of their happiness behind.

Jo had been right when she'd said that this house had the ability to heal. In this house, around the Ballantynes, she felt happier, centered, more focused. She felt like she was home.

Tate heard footsteps behind her and twisted her torso to look up the stairs. Linc stood at the top of the stairs staring at her with a strange look on his face.

"I thought you were downstairs."

"I took Ellie up to Sage and grabbed something from my room."

The odd look on his face remained as he looked at her.

"What's the matter?" Tate demanded. "Are the kids okay?"

Linc shook his head as if to clear it and half jogged down the stairs. "Shaw is still asleep, Ellie is cuddling with Sage."

Tate started to stand up, but Linc's hand on her shoulder kept her butt glued to the stair. "No, stay there," he said. "This spot is as good as any."

"To do what?"

"This." Linc sat down next her and immediately pulled her to him and started to kiss her, his hand going to her breast. Tate laughed and pulled back.

"I'm fairly adventurous, Ballantyne, but your sister is upstairs and might need to use these stairs," Tate drily told him. "And your siblings all have a key to that front door, and they frequently use it, and at odd times, too."

Linc grinned, and then his face turned serious. "Does that bother you?"

"Does what bother me?"

"Does it bother you that The Den is Grand Central Station? I love this house, but if it doesn't suit you, if you want something more private, then we can move."

"I love your house, Linc. I don't want to live anywhere else."

Linc smiled. "I want this house to be ours, Tate, the kids will ours, that we do this together as equal partners. We *can* have it all. It'll be crazy trying to juggle two careers, the kids, but I'm convinced we can fuse it all together into one glorious mess."

"Yours, mine...ours." Tate pushed the words out between her lips, stunned once again by his generosity, love bubbling in her stomach. She placed her hand on his hard thigh and rested her forehead on his shoulder. "Yeah, I think we can do that. But The Den, this is where I want to live."

She heard Linc's relieved sigh and felt the kiss he pressed into her hair. Tate didn't want to move; she just wanted to sit here, listening to the house and inhaling Linc's sexy, citrusy cologne.

"I love you, Linc," she whispered, pushing herself over the last barrier between them.

"You, Shaw and Ellie and the kids… What we have together will always be the center of my world, the reason the earth spins for me," she added, her voice low and intense. So much emotion swirled between them, but Tate finally embraced her passionate feelings instead of bolting from them. "I don't love often, Linc, but when I do, I love with everything I have. I'll always love you."

"I love you, too, sweetheart," Linc replied, his voice husky. "Come here."

Tate scooted onto his lap, straddling him, his thighs hard under hers. She held his face in her hands and looked into his mesmerizing eyes, happy to see laughter and contentment brimming in those stunning gray depths.

"Love you," she murmured, desperate to tell him again.

Linc jerked her toward him, and his mouth covered hers, demanding that she translate that emotion into her kiss. Tate was more than happy to oblige, and within minutes she was chest to chest with Linc, rubbing the juncture between her legs against his rock-hard erection. Her hands pushed under his sweater and shirt, needing his skin on hers, desperate to show him how much she loved him, desired him, how much her body had missed his.

The door behind them opened, and Tate heard an outburst of laughter as far too many Ballantynes crowded into the hallway. Tate pulled back and lifted her eyebrows at Linc.

Linc sent her a half amused, half sour look. "They thought I might need help talking you into staying."

"Guess we weren't needed after all," Jaeger stated.

Tate looked over her shoulder. Yep, the entire clan, Jaeger and Piper, Beck and Cady and Reame were standing in the hallway, watching them with open amusement.

"Have you guys heard about this new thing they've invented?" Beck asked, shedding his coat and throwing it on the pile that was building on the settee. "It's called a bedroom. And you have impressionable kids in the house."

"And Sage is here," Jaeger added.

Tate looked from one sibling's face to the next, and in the eyes of each, she saw that they were happy for Linc, that she was now part of this crazy, extended family. They liked her, they approved of her, and they might, in time, come to love her. Her eyes collided with Reame's, and he winked at her.

Tate turned back to Linc, and, staying on his lap, she decided to mess with his cocky siblings. "Linc, does the conversation we've just had mean that I am the de facto mistress of The Den?"

Linc, because he knew her so well, immediately picked up on the teasing in her voice, but he kept his face bland. "Yep. Pretty much." He pushed his hand into his pocket and pulled out Connor's ring, the color a deep, happy green. "Though if you agree to wear this ring, we'd make that, and a bunch of other things, legal."

Tate ignored Cady and Piper's squeals, keeping her eyes on Linc's beloved face. "Is that a proposal, Linc?" she asked, amused.

"Sure is." He smiled. "If you agree to marry me, to stay with me for the next sixty or so years, it comes with the added bonus of becoming mistress of The Den and bossing that lot around."

So happy, Tate thought. She didn't know she could feel this full, so blissful.

"Only sixty years? I think we can do better than that," she replied with a radiant smile.

"Is that a yes?" Linc asked with a catch in his voice.

"Yes, that's a yes! I love you, and I can't think of anything more I'd like to do than spend the rest of my life with you." Tate said, dropping a soft kiss on Linc's mouth. She lifted her head and grinned. "But bossing your siblings around holds a certain appeal."

"Go away," she told Linc's family—no, her family— smiling as she tossed a look over her shoulder toward their audience. "I have plans for your brother."

Nobody was more surprised than her when all of them picked up their coats. Reame grabbed the door handle, and Tate watched, utterly astounded as they started walking out of The Den.

Tate immediately felt bad. She'd been joking, dammit! She started to call them back when Linc clapped his hand over her mouth, his face suffused with laughter. "Good job at getting rid of them, sweet-heart."

"I was joking!" Tate wailed. "Make them come back!"

"Not a chance in hell," Linc muttered, standing up with her in his arms. "Because I have plans for my brand-new fiancée. Naked plans."

Tate sent another look at the door, biting her bottom lip. "But—they—"

Linc rolled his eyes, placed her on her feet and jogged to the front door. Yanking it open, he shouted to his family who were halfway to the sidewalk. "Come back for dinner! Bring food!"

Linc slammed the door behind him and slapped his hands on his hips, looking down at Tate with one sexy eyebrow raised. "Happy now?"

Tate ran the tip of her finger down the long ridge in his pants. "I will be."

"Damn right you will be," Linc growled. "I'll race you to the bedroom. You get a five-second start."

Tate started running up the steps, and as she hit the landing she nearly barreled into Shaw. He immediately launched himself at her legs. "Tate! You're back! I missed you! Spike missed you. Come say hi to Spike. I played the drums at school…"

"For God's sake," Linc muttered, shoving a frustrated hand into his hair.

Tate, her arm around Shaw's shoulder, laughed out loud when she saw Sage walking down the stairs from the third floor, carrying Ellie. When she met Tate on the landing, Sage immediately noticed Linc's ring on her finger and lifted it up to take a better look. "Oh, my God! Is that Connor's ring? Are you going to marry him?"

Tate grinned down at Linc at the bottom of the stairs, her eyes on his as Shaw tugged at her arm and Ellie moved from Sage's arms to hers. "I so am."

With an arm around Shaw's shoulders and holding her best girl, Tate laughed before saying, "Since everyone is awake, do you want to call the rest of the clan back, Linc?"

"Might as well," he grumbled, hands on his hips and looking frustrated. "Bloody madhouse. I think we should move out."

Tate laughed again and shook her head. "Not a chance. I love this house, our children and you."

Linc's eyes softened, and Tate noticed his Adam's apple bob in his throat. "I love you more."

He lifted his phone out of his pocket and texted his brothers and Reame. When he was done, his eyes moved from Tate and his kids, to his sister.

He smiled, looking relaxed and happy. "Happy to have another brother off your hands, Sage? And, I'd like it noted, that you didn't even have to pay Tate to get rid of me."

Sage nodded, but Tate noticed the tender emotion in her eyes. "I might reward her by redesigning Connor's ring. It's a little old-fashioned. As for taking you off my hands, I have to admit that you are fractionally less annoying than my other two brothers."

Linc winked at Tate before looking at Sage, his expression contemplative. "And that raises the question—how are we going to get *you* off *our* hands?"

Tate placed her hand on Sage's shoulder. "And that's brotherspeak for him, us, hoping that you, too, will find love, Sage."

Sage groaned and covered her face with her hands. *"Ugh."*

Linc cocked his head. "So, what exactly is going on between you and Latimore, Sage?" he asked, gray eyes teasing.

Sage threw her hands up in the air and scowled. "I swear my guardian angel was drunk when she put that man in my path."

Tate kissed Ellie's head and squeezed Shaw's shoulder. Looking down at her man, she smiled, utterly in love. Frankly, if her guardian angel was responsible for all her happy, she was doing a hell of a job and deserved a raise.

* * * * *

If you liked this sassy, sexy story from Joss Wood,
pick up her other Harlequin Desire novels!

TRAPPED WITH THE MAVERICK MILLIONAIRE
PREGNANT BY THE MAVERICK MILLIONAIRE
MARRIED TO THE MAVERICK MILLIONAIRE

And the first of the
BALLANTYNE BILLIONAIRES *series,*
HIS EX'S WELL-KEPT SECRET

Available now from Harlequin Desire!

***

And don't miss the next
BILLIONAIRES AND BABIES *story,*
A FAMILY FOR THE BILLIONAIRE

by Dani Wade.
Available September 2017!

***

If you're on Twitter, tell us what you think of
Harlequin Desire! #harlequindesire

COMING NEXT MONTH FROM

Available August 8, 2017

#2533 THE CEO'S NANNY AFFAIR
Billionaires and Babies • by Joss Wood
When billionaire Linc Ballantyne's ex abandons not one, but *two* children, he strikes up a wary deal with her too-sexy sister. She'll be the nanny and they'll keep their hands to themselves. But their temporary truce soon becomes a temporary tryst!

#2534 TEMPTED BY THE WRONG TWIN
Texas Cattleman's Club: Blackmail • by Rachel Bailey
Harper Lake is pregnant, but the father isn't who she thinks—it's her boss's identical twin brother! Wealthy former Navy SEAL Nick Tate pretended to be his brother as a favor, and now he's proposing a marriage of convenience that just might lead to real romance...

#2535 THE TEXAN'S BABY PROPOSAL
Callahan's Clan • by Sara Orwig
Millionaire Texan Marc Medina must marry immediately to inherit his grandfather's ranch. When his newly single secretary tells him she's pregnant, he knows a brilliant deal when he sees one. He'll make her his wife...and have her in his bed!

#2536 LITTLE SECRETS: CLAIMING HIS PREGNANT BRIDE by Sarah M. Anderson
Restless—that's businessman and biker Seth Bolton. But when he rescues pregnant runaway bride Kate Burroughs, he wants much more than he should with the lush mom-to-be... But she won't settle for anything less than taming his heart!

#2537 FROM TEMPTATION TO TWINS
Whiskey Bay Brides • by Barbara Dunlop
When Juliet Parker goes home to reopen her grandfather's restaurant, she clashes with her childhood crush, tycoon Caleb Watford, who's building a rival restaurant. Then the stakes skyrocket after their one night leaves her expecting two little surprises!

#2538 THE TYCOON'S FIANCÉE DEAL
The Wild Caruthers Bachelors • by Katherine Garbera
Derek Caruthers promised his best friend that their fake engagement would end after he'd secured his promotion...but what's a man of honor to do when their red-hot kisses prove she's the only one for him?

Get 2 Free Books,
Plus 2 Free Gifts—
just for trying the Reader Service!

Violet, looking messier than Hogan had ever seen her, was leaning over the papers again scattered across her desk.

"Violet?"

Slowly she turned her face toward him.

Her bloodshot eyes surprised him. Sick. He stepped in farther. "Hey, you okay?"

She looked from him to the paperwork. "I don't know." More coughs racked her.

Hogan strode forward and put a hand to her forehead. "Shit. You're burning up."

"What time is it?"

"A few minutes after midnight."

"Oh." She pushed back from the desk but didn't make it far. "The restaurant," she gasped in between strained breaths.

"I took care of it." Holding her elbow, he helped to support her as she stood. His most pressing thought was getting her home and in bed. No, not the way he'd like, but definitely the way she needed. "Where are your car keys?"

Unsteady on her feet, she frowned. "What do you mean, you took care of it?"

"You have good employees—you know that. They're aware of the routine. Colt pitched in, too. Everything is done."

"But…"

"I double-checked. I'm not incompetent, so trust me."

Her frown darkened.

"You can thank me, Violet."

She tried to look stern, coughed again and gave up. "Thank you." Still she kept one hand on the desk. "I'm just so blasted tired."

"I know." He eased her into his side, his arm around her. "Come on. Let me drive you home." Then he found her purse and without a qualm, dug through it for her keys.

He found them. He also found two condoms. His gaze flashed to hers, but her eyes were closed and she looked asleep on her feet, her body utterly boneless as she drew in shallow, strained breaths.

"Come on." With an arm around her, her purse and keys held in his free hand, he led her out the back way to the employee lot, securing the door behind her. Her yellow Mustang shone bright beneath security lights.

His bike would be okay. Or at least, it better be.

Violet tried to get herself together but it wasn't easy. She honestly felt like she could close her eyes and nod right off. "The trash—"

"Was taken out." He opened the passenger door and helped her in.

"If you left on even one fan—"

"It would set off the security sensors. I know. They're all off." He fastened her seat belt around her and closed her door.

As soon as he slid behind the wheel, she said, "But the end-of-day reports—"

"Are done." He started her car. "Try not to worry, okay?"

Easier said than done.

Because the town was so small, Hogan seemed to know where she lived even though she'd never had him over. She hadn't dared.

Hogan in her home? Nope. Not a good idea.

Even feeling miserable, her head pounding and her chest aching, she was acutely aware of him beside her in the enclosed car, and the way he kept glancing at her. He tempted her, always had, from the first day she'd met him.

He was also a major runaround. Supposedly a reformed runaround, but she didn't trust in that. Things had happened with his late wife, things that had made him bitter and unpredictable.

Yet no less appealing.

She wasn't one to pry; otherwise she might have gotten all the details from Honor, his sister-in-law, already. She figured if he ever wanted to, Hogan himself would tell her. Not that there was any reason, since she would not get involved with him.

Hogan was fun to tease, like watching the flames in a bonfire. You watched, you enjoyed, but you did not jump in the fire. She needed Hogan Guthrie, but she wasn't a stupid woman, so she tried to never court trouble.

Don't miss WORTH THE WAIT
by New York Times *bestselling author Lori Foster!*

HARLEQUIN® *Desire*

AVAILABLE SEPTEMBER 2017

CONVENIENT CINDERELLA BRIDE

BY

JOSS WOOD,

PART OF THE SIZZLING

SECRETS OF THE A-LIST

SERIES

Prince Charming—With Strings Attached

Billionaire playboy Jonas Halstead has exactly ninety days to marry—or be cut off from his family's hotel dynasty. What he needs is a practical, like-minded woman who isn't looking to be swept off her feet.

Jonah's seductive offer could save Katrina Morrison from financial ruin. But how can she be his wife in name only with desire tempting them to break the rules of their strictly hands-off arrangement? As passion complicates the journey to "I do," will Kat lose her heart to the man she's agreed to honor and cherish for however long their temporary marriage may last?

Preorder your copy today!

HDALIST2017